Kicked Out
The Player's Club

ISBN 978-1-956793-03-1

Table of Contents

Dirty Dick.   3

Gullible.   11

Baby Mama Drama.   22

What They Don't Know.   33

D.L Dilemma.   42

What Goes Around...   52

Musical Chairs.   64

Liar, Liar.   73

The Sacrifices We Make.   85

A Bitch Named Carmen (Karma)   95

Keno's Story   107

Intro...

I see so many women writing, blogging, and posting about the problems or issues they have with us men. How their man cheated, "won't change", or refuses to settle down. It makes me laugh to see some of the stuff the ladies are saying because half the time, they are the root to their own issues with us. I'm not saying that women are 100 percent to blame; I'm just saying... take some responsibility in your decisions and roll in the situation... hell, at least your selection process! I'm not even supposed to be giving the game away like this but I had to step in.

I got some of the fellas together to tell some of their situations so I can point out what the real issues are. Then, after I've dropped a few secrets and gems on you, I'm going to tell my own story. These are stories you won't believe; a story filled with love, betrayal, deceit, friendship, failure, and of course sexual experiences that even my boys and couldn't believe we had. They are guaranteed to start a debate about who was in the wrong. Ladies don't shoot the messenger. I'm just being honest... I'm about to get Kicked Out The Player's Club for this one....

"We might as well just pick days, dealing with your dirty dick ass."
-A bitter woman who's staying anyway

Dirty Dick

Not every time we do some dirty shit is our fault. For example, one time, I had this situation occur. This chick from work that was always throw the pussy at me was at it like usual.

"Why not? You think you can't handle it?" The words slipped effortlessly from her red lipstick covered lips.

I looked her in the eyes, debating my next move in my head. I let my eyes scan her body and she leaned in and whispered.

"I know you like what you see." She grazed her long nails over the growing bulge in my pants. "It's obvious. So, what's stopping you from getting what I know both of us want?"

"You drove?" I mumbled.

"Yeah."

"Aight, follow me." I walked off, stopping only to say my goodbyes to a few of the fellas.

"Be safe, man." One of them told me with a laugh and a glance in her direction.

"Always." I said, looking at her and letting all the things I could do to her run away with my thoughts.

Fifteen minutes later, her round ass bounced up and down on my lap making wet and loud slapping sounds. The shower water ran down over my shoulders and splashed off her body as we moved; so, everything was wet...but her pussy was wetter.

"Shit!" I moaned as I pulled her waist towards me for a deep stroke.

She smiled because she knew the pussy was good, but I knew the dick was hitting different when she started to cum.

"Ahhh! Oh my Go--!!" She screamed, motivating me to stand up.

The big walk-in shower in our hotel room was our first and only stop. Everything else was still untouched. I bent her over and stroked like I knew I would never fuck her again...shit, I hadn't planned on fucking her this time; but when she threw that pussy at me for what felt like the 50th time, I had to catch it. With that being said...I love my wife; so, this would be the first and last time. I had to make it good.

"I knew… mmmmm... I knew this dick was going to be... mmmmm... good." She said between moans.

"Shut up and cum on this dick again." I slapped her ass.

"Shit! Yes, daddy!" She screamed and began bouncing her ass to the rhythm of my hard strokes.

I felt a knot in my stomach and knew I was going cum; so, I stroked harder to make her cum again first. Her legs began to shake and her knees buckled just a little but I held that ass up.

"Un-un. Hold this shit up. I'm about buss." I hissed at her still fucking her hard until she her got down on her knees; I followed right behind her.

4

Water sprayed over my head, but I didn't need to see to reach my destination. I stroked until I felt the knot in my stomach travel down into my nuts then up toward the head of my throbbing hard dick. Then I snatched out and bussed all over her back.

"Fuck!" I yelled, cumming much harder than I expected.

We got out of the shower and I expected to leave but she got down on her knees in front of me and looked up like a begging puppy. I put my dick in her throat just because of the look she gave me.

She sucked the head of my shit like she thought I might cum gold. Before I knew it, I was tossing her ass onto the bed and diving back in as far as my dick could reach.

I was stroking like that pussy had diamonds in the bottom of it and when she started to shake again, I felt it squeeze my dick so tight that I had to push her ass off me so I wouldn't cum inside her.

"Come suck this muthafucka." I commanded.

She did as she was told so eagerly that I was shooting cum down the back of her throat in under a minute.

I backed away and got dressed as she curled up under the sheets.

"You leaving?" She purred.

"Yeah."

"We should do this again some time." She smiled slyly.

"Umhm." Was all I gave her as I grabbed my keys.

"Call me." She said to my back with a giggle right before the door slammed shut.

I hopped into my car and sped off but slowed down as I turned onto my street. I glanced at the clock in the dash. 12:37. It was still early, I had nothing to worry about.

I pulled in front of the house and sat for a few minutes. No particular reason, just a habit I had developed. I got out and walked the stairs to the front door. Music came floating out as I opened it.

"Dedicating this one to my favorite girrrl. She's the only woman in the worrrrld..." R Kelly and Public Announcement crooned the through the surround sound speakers.

The smell of vanilla hit my nose and I immediately thought of the candles Tiffany had begged me to pay $30 for at Bath and Bodyworks two days before.

She came into the living room in a money green Victoria Secret lace panty and bra set. Her black and gold satin robe hung loosely and open around her.

"Hey, baby." She smiled as she walked over to me on her painted white toes.

"Hey, baby." I replied as I put my keys, phone and wallet down on the side table.

"I've been waiting for you." She added; kissing my lips with a peck at first. Then she came in for a second kiss...this one was longer and deeper and she ended up sucking my tongue between her lips.

"Wait, baby." I said, pulling away gently. "It's been a long day. Let me jump in the shower."

She ignored me; kissing on my neck because she knew it would get her what she wanted.

"Tiff, wait." I grabbed her hands gently and held them away from my pants.

She bit my neck and mumbled, "Please." The vibration of her voice on my neck betrayed me.

"I'm not saying no... just wait." I mumbled.

She kept sucking my neck and my dick grew...despite my best efforts to keep him down. I put my hands on her waist and she slid them down to cuff her soft ass.

"For what? Up." She demanded. I picked her up and she wrapped her legs around me.

"I just want to hop in the shower. You can get in with me."

She kissed me again and began to grind her pussy against me. She broke our kiss and said, "I want it now. Feel how wet she is...I been waiting for you."

I sat her on the island in the kitchen and let my fingers find their way to her pearl. She pussy lips were soaked with her excitement.

"See? Don't you want it?"

For a second, I fell into it; then I remembered how wet shorty from work was and I knew I had to wash my dick first. "I got you...I promise. Just ten minutes." I told her, only wanting to get some hot soapy water on my dick and balls anyway.

She huffed and pushed me away and got down off the island. I thought she gave up; until she dropped down to her knees in front of me. She unbuttoned my pants and I panicked, but thought quickly on my feet.

I bent down and scooped her up, then sat her on the island again and got down on my knees between her legs. Her full lips curled into a smile as I pulled her panties to the side. I licked and sucked on her wetness until she was pushing my head away.

"Now, fuck me." She demanded.

I shook my head, but the disbelief on her face let me know that I had to either do it or explain why I didn't want to fuck her for the first time ever after eating her pussy like that. So, I pulled my dick out and she pulled me inside her. She held me tightly as I slow-stroked her and kissed her lips, face and neck.

We fucked for 40 minutes and yeah...it was good; but my mind kept going back to how dirty my dick was. We came together, me inside her and her all over my dick. Afterward, I pulled slowly out of her and backed away.

"What's wrong?" She looked me in the eyes and suddenly felt self-conscious. She closed her legs and reached between them to adjust her panties. Then she tilted her head and squinted her eyes.

"Nothing. I'm going to take a shower." I left her sitting there without a clue.

Keno Said It...

A person who would attempt to use a superior position to obtain sexual favors from a subordinate could be described as a sexual manipulator. People like this are sexually aggressive; usually their objective is their own sexual gratification. They have no concern for the best interests of the other person, and tend to be driven by their own fantasies and need for sexual control as they manipulate and take advantage of a partner... any partner... as their focus one person is most often short.

"You really think I'm stupid, don't you?"

-A woman who will fall for whatever

Gullible

"I didn't mean what I said." She moaned as I held her head down with one hand and pulled her fat ass back into my strokes.

"Yes, you did." I said without missing a beat.

"I was just mad." She whined, clearly struggling to take all of my dick.

"Well, I'm mad now. What should I do about it?" I paused, holding my dick as far inside her as it would reach.

"Ahh! I'm sorry."

"No, you're not...not yet." I leaned in and kissed the middle of her back. Then I put both hands on her waist and stroked hard and fast.

"I'm sorry I said that!" She screamed. " I didn't mean it!"

"Say it to me now." I demanded in a low even tone.

She hesitated; so, I pulled back and stroked as hard as my hips and her round ass would let me.

"I hope I never see you again." She whimpered.

"Say it again." I hissed down at her; getting a little angrier than even I expected.

"I- I hope- I hope I never see-" She struggled to speak between my strokes.

"Say it."

"I hope I never see you again!" She cried out, but her body buckled under me and I knew she was cumming.

I kept stroking until I came, then slid out of her. I gave her a tap on the ass on my way to flush the condom, then I got dressed.

"You leaving?" She looked like she might cry.

"Yeah, you hoped you never see me again. You know I always give what you want." I grabbed my jacket and walked out of her bedroom. Then out of her life.

You can always tell what kind of woman you're dealing with...especially if you know women like I do. I knew she wasn't a keeper, so I just kept things physical. That way it was easy to walk when I needed to. I'm not saying this to brag, but I know women. That's why women are so drawn to me. I know them, I know what they want. I know what to say and how to act to get them to do, say, or be whatever I want. With that being said, I knew exactly what kind of woman Briana was the day I met her.

She parked next to me outside of my favorite Jamaican restaurant. I was on the phone with a friend of mine at the time, so I didn't notice her right away.

"When you coming to see me? This pussy been missing you." While the idea sparked my interest, her voice annoyed me.

"I don't know; I'ma see." I lied. I knew damn well I had no plans of going to see her any time soon. I hate a needy female.

I looked out my window as she parked and she happened to be looking my way at the same time. I ended my call. "Let me call you right back."

"You better call me back too." She sucked her teeth.

"I got you." I kept looking over at her; but by this time, she was getting her shit together to get out the car. I hopped out first and purposely stood by my car.

"Excuse me." She said as she squeezed her fat ass between our cars. She gave me a weak smile, then got who I later found out was her son out of his seat in the back.

I watched her take her son by the hand, then glance my way and flash another weak smile. I could tell she was shy and found that to be sweet- if it wasn't an act. *I mean who is still shy?* Anyway, I hurried over to hold door open for her.

"Thank you." She purred and blushed.

"My pleasure." I smiled and stole another quick glance at her ass.

It looked soft as hell as it bounced slightly with every step. I immediately saw myself bending that ass over in my mind.

I got behind her in line and she kept glancing back at me, but wouldn't say anything. So, after her third time looking back, I shot my shot. "You got a man?" I said, getting straight to the point.

"Excuse me?" She turned to face me, trying to hide her smile.

I looked her in the eyes. "You're beautiful. Do you have a man?" I flashed her a slick grin.

"You tryna be him?" She surprised me... not as shy as I thought.

"Is the position open?" I shot back.

"Yeah." She tilted her head as she looked up at me.

I looked down at her son and nodded in his direction. "He yours?"

"Yes."

"Any more?" The most important question so far.

"No, just him."

I let my eyes roam the length of her body.

"Like what you see?"

"Umhmm." I nodded. "Call my phone."

We exchanged numbers and went our separate ways, but she called me later that night. We talked for a bit and made plans to link.

Like I said, I knew right away what type of woman she was...so, I took her out a few times before she would lay down for me. I wasn't even mad because the first time proved to be worth the wait.

We went to a little comedy show and afterward, we ended up back at her spot. I sat on the couch thinking she was going to pour us a night cap and send me on my way like before. I was too surprised when she came back into the living room wearing this lace royal blue panty set that made my mouth water. Don't get me wrong, the dresses she wore on our dates showed me she had curves, but seeing it all in the flesh was a whole different ball game. Her full breasts sat perky in the bra and her chocolate nipples played peek-a-boo in the lace fabric. The matching boy shorts put the entire bottom of her ass on display. Her thick thighs were the icing on the cake and you have to know I wanted more than a slice.

"Come on." She nodded her head toward the bedroom and reached out for my hand.

I took her hand and let her lead the way. I watched all of her move seductively in front of me and made plans for all the positions I was about to put her in.

We entered the bedroom and she closed the door behind us. She had 90's r&b playing softly and sweet-smelling candles lit. The whole setup was a vibe.

"Lay down." I took charge.

She lowered herself back onto the bed slowly. "Um..." she began nervously. "I've thought a lot about this and I want us to be together."

"I see." I nodded.

"So... are we?" The little confidence she had mustered to make this move was obvious shaky.

"Let me show you." I told her, flashing a half grin.

I laid down beside her and kissed her lips... softly, like one of those 90's black romance movie kisses.

I kissed my way down to her 36Cs and gave each nipple my full attention. I sucked each one softly and twirled my tongue around them before kissing a trail down to her belly button. I licked it and kissed it and nibbled on each of her hips. She put her hand on the top of my head, trying to gently push me to my destination. I looked up at her and took both of her wrists into one hand, holding them together on her stomach as I kissed her pearl and she gasped for air.

Ten minutes later, she was mushing my head away while her legs shook on my shoulders. I popped my head up. "You had enough?"

"Y-yes." She moaned.

"You sure? I'll keep going if you ask me to." I smirked, knowing damn well she couldn't take another lick.

"I'm sure." She whimpered.

"You ready for this dick?" I asked the obvious, letting my breath hit her clit as I spoke.

She closed her eyes. "Yes, I'm ready."

"Say please." I teased her.

"Please." She purred.

I pulled myself up and repositioned myself on top of her. I stared her in the eyes as I eased my hardness into her. She slowly exhaled.

I started out with slow, long strokes because she was so wet. I had to make a lasting impression, so I lifted her legs onto my shoulders and stroked her like I was apologizing and she eagerly accepted every inch I was putting down.

16

"Oh my God!" Her moans echo around us. "It's so good!"

"Say it again." I demanded and stroked deeper.

"It's... soooo...good." she repeated between strokes.

"This dick yours?" I asked her.

"Umhmm." She mumbled.

"I can't hear you." I put my hands on her ankles and gave her every inch in one hard stroke.

"It's mine!" She screamed.

"Then cum on it." I demanded.

That was how damn near every night after that went. I'd make my money, then link with her and put my whole dick in her back. Then I'd kiss it to make it feel better.

It went like that for months, seasons even. Summer came and went and so did winter. Before I knew it, we had created a nice little routine. Spending time together, me taking her out on dates and even doing things with her son. I could tell she felt safe with me because she was opening up more.

"I was thinking about investing a little. I mean, I don't really know what else to do when that tax money hits." She confessed for the tenth time in the last few weeks.

I listened attentively. "Well, why don't we go into business together." I suggested (like I said, I knew what I had in her).

"Really?" She squealed. "It's supposed to hit at midnight. We have to have a good plan."

The rest of the car ride was spent talking about different businesses we could start together.

When we got to her house that night, we ate and put her son to sleep. Then, it was play time.

She was in the bathroom getting ready for me when she said, "I don't know why you don't just move in here. You spend almost every night here anyway." She came out completely naked and unashamed. "I mean, I never even been to your place."

"That's because we agreed that me coming here is easier for you being that you have your son." I reminded her.

"I know. I'm just saying...at least bring a few things over." She shrugged as she climbed onto my lap.

"I'll think about it." I agreed. Then I took her chin in two of my fingers and kissed her lips. "You know I like him sucked first."

"I know." She smiled a sexy grin. Then kissed her way down.

She sucked my dick deep into her throat and I closed my eyes to fully enjoy the feeling. She twirled her tongue against my shaft as she came up and slurped hard and she let me slide to the back of her throat over and over again. Every few minutes, she wrapped her lips around the head and sucked on it like her favorite flavor lollipop. I put my hand on her head and guided her back down to suck my whole dick but she kept making her way to my head and this is what usually got me. Every time I came in her mouth, I came so hard. This time was not different. I held her head down gently and shot what felt like my soul into the softest part of her mouth- the very back where her throat begins.

She sucked every drop of my cum out of me. Then got up feeling like the undisputed champ.

"My turn." Was all I said to her.

I pushed her legs back and sucked her clit like when she came, it would be liquid gold. I licked and sucked until she came kicking and screaming all over my tongue, lips, and chin. Then I held her legs down and started over. I let her cum on my tongue four more times and kept going. I didn't stop until I felt like I might cum with her if she came again. Then I put my dick in her heart with every stroke.

When I finally came and rolled off of her, I was covered in sweat and she curled into the fetus position, holding her knees because she was shaking and cumming uncontrollably.

As if on que, her phone pinged. She reached over and peaked at it. "The money dropped." She whispered.

"Okay." I said, brushing it off. "I'm tired. Come here so we can fall asleep."

She laid her head on my chest and we both fell asleep. The next morning, we talked again about the plan we came up with.

It really was a good plan. Shit, I still might do it now that I have the money… but not with her because she hasn't heard from my ass in a month. New number, who this?

Like I said, I knew the type of woman she was when I met her...a gullible one.

Keno Said It...

Here Are 6 Signs That sweet talking nigga ain't shit ...

• · He's *not interested* in getting to know shit about you.

• He's *closed off* about himself, you don't know shit about him but his name and what store he likes to shop in.

• Your *conversations are basic*, and mostly about how fucked up his day was.

• He *doesn't include you* in his life. He will tell you him and the boys going to kick it; you later on see post on social media and it looks like couple's night at a circus and he's the only clown without his lady.

• He *doesn't care how you feel*, you express small things like visiting your sick mom and he says weird shit like, "how you going to your mother house and didn't cook shit yet?"

• You've *never met anyone he knows*, not even the dad that obviously didn't teach this boy shit about being a man.

• He's *requesting too many favors*, starting off with small shit like a ride, but quickly escalating to borrowing your car and needing that rent money for a few days.

• He's *reluctance to compromise*, everything about this lame is one sided; he actually thinks the term "ladies before gentlemen" is an explanation on who should pay the bills and take care of the house.

"Every baby daddy still fucks his baby mama."

-A baby mama who will always let her baby daddy fuck.

Baby Mama Drama

I love my woman. I think she is one of the best choices I've made in a long time. That's why every day around lunch, I stop whatever I'm doing to fuck her. At first, it was just because I couldn't get enough; but now it's more because she mentioned it the couple days I didn't do it. Don't get me wrong, the pussy is still just as good. I just don't like strict routines, and Tameka is the queen of those. So, I was on my way to the house to drop some dick off.

"Tameka! Come here right quick, I have to make a run before I come in for the night." I called to her as I peeled off a few bills to give her.

"I don't even need all of that." She said as she walked into the living room.

"Do you need all of this?" I said, pulling her against my hard dick.

"Oooh. I need all of that." She said before kissing my lips lightly.

I slid my tongue into her mouth and let her suck on it how she liked to do.

"Um." She pulled away gently. "Don't try to distract me, James. What run you have to make before you come in for the night?" She tried to escape my grip on her waist but I just held her tighter.

22

"Come here." I demanded and slid one hand down to caress her clit over her stretch pants.

"Mmmm." She moaned.

"The question is... where the hell you going in these pants and no panties?" I slapped her ass. It wasn't the fattest...but it was definitely a handful.

"Nowhere." She mumbled as I started to suck on her neck.

"Um. Get that ass to the room."

Five minutes later, I was gripping her waist as she bounced on my lap. I could feel her cum dripping down between us but I wasn't finished yet. So, I made her keep bouncing.

"Oh my God!" She screamed. "You make your pussy feel so good."

"Long as you know this is my pussy." I let her know and turned her over onto her back while using my knee to bend one of her legs. I managed to keep that dick deep in her as we moved because she loved that move.

"Well, if it's yours...make this muthafucka cum." She looked me in my eyes.

"You say that like you ain't dripping that gushy shit all over this dick every night and most mornings." I pulled myself up onto my knees.

"I said what I said." She teased.

For the next half hour, I made her take those words back; and when I was done, she had no objections to whatever I was leaving to go do.

"I'm cooking. So, let me know if you'll be out late." She said as she walked me to the door.

"I can do that." I agreed.

"Be safe." It was sweet. She said the same thing to me every time I left her since the first time she let me lay her down.

"I always am." I assure her. "See you later." I kissed her lips. "Lock the door."

"Okay. Love you." She said.

"I love you more." I said back and walked out.

I can't say that I feel bad for what I did next because it wasn't the first time. I'll just say I regret how things played put because of it.

My phone rang as soon as I closed the door to my car and I couldn't stop myself from smiling big as I answered. "Perfect timing."

"If that's true, you must be on your way to me." She replied.

"Be there in 15." I told her.

"I want it soon as you walk in." She purred.

Fifteen minutes later, I was pulling up at her house. I won't lie, it was a different feeling going to see her back then. My dick would be hard before I walked through the door.

When I walked in, she dropped to her knees in front of me. It wasn't until then that I remembered that I still had my wife all over me.

I should have stopped her, but I didn't. She unzipped my pants and took me into her mouth. Immediately, she spit me out. "You so disrespectful! You come to me so I can have her sloppy seconds."

I held back a laugh... she said that as if she wasn't my side chick. I could have stopped her and washed it first but let's be real...she was my side chick. All of the attitude was unnecessary.

"I could slap that smirk off your face." She sucked her teeth and got up.

"Yeah, okay. You know better than that. Just go get a soapy rag and wash it for me. You used to do that with no problem." I follow her to the bedroom.

"Oh, it's no problem for me." She said and started the shower. She washed my entire like I had fallen into some poison.

After we got out, she sucked my dick better than she ever had. I felt like I was having a fucking out of body experience. Then she insisted on putting on the condom for me.

I reluctantly agreed. "Only if you put it on with your mouth like you did before."

She did and arched that fat ass high in the air for me to get behind. I did my thing, left her ass fast asleep when I walked out.

For the next three months, shit went smooth. I kept both of my ladies happy. Both were getting time with me and of course money. So, neither of them had a single complaint. I was living my best life; or so I thought until Sherika called me over randomly one day. I figured she was just upset because I had been home a little more with Tameka. She hadn't been feeling well. So, after a week and a half...I took her to the hospital. Turns out, she was pregnant but had to be put on bed-rest. So, I had been spending a little more time taking care of her.

I got to Sherika's place and she was crying. I mean, balling. Face soaked and nose running. I had never seen her like that before.

"What's wrong?" I asked her. Pulling her onto my lap after taking a seat on the couch.

"I'm not doing it." She shook her head. "I don't care what you say."

"You're not doing what?" I had no idea what the fuck she was talking about.

"I'm not getting rid of my baby." She buried her face in my neck.

"Your what?" I couldn't believe my ears. *What the fuck was I going to do with another baby on the way?*

"I'm pregnant, Rick; and we're having a baby because I'm not about to go lay up on nobody chop-shop table. Don't ask me to do that."

I sat there quiet for a minute thinking, *what the fuck.*

"Rick?!" She sounded far away because my thought already had me at home with Tameka. *How the hell was I going to tell her?* "Rick?!" She called again.

"Yes." I mumbled.

"Say something." She pleaded.

"What do you want me to say?" I looked her in the eyes.

"Say you want me to keep our baby. Reassure me that everything will be fine. I don't know! Say whatever the fuck you said to Tameka when you found out her bony ass was pregnant!"

I pushed her gently off my lap. "You stay bringing her up. You knew when we started that I had somebody. Comparing yourself to her ass ain't gonna get you shit but mad. So, cut it the fuck out." I let her know as calmly as I could manage. Then I added, "About this baby...I can't tell you what to do with yo body. You sound like your mind is made up...so, I have to just rock with what you already decided. How far are you?"

"Hm... you sure the fuck do. Four months. So... You gonna tell her about our little bundle of joy, or should I?" She said with an attitude and not a single tear in sight.

I got up. "Neither one if us telling her shit. I gotta make a run...hit me if you need me." I had to get the hell out of there. I needed some air to process that shit. Two babies on the way by two different women.

"A run? I bet if I had called offering you this pussy and throat...yo ass wouldn't have no runs to make."

I left her house feeling fucked up. Rethinking the decision I made to fuck around. I just knew Tameka was gonna kill me.

I made a little more money then went to the house to check on Tameka. She was crying and packing when I walk in.

"You stupid muthafucka!" She screamed when she saw me.

"Baby, what the fuck you doing? The doctor said you need to be laying down."

"Fuck that doctor, fuck that bed, and fuck you!" She grabbed a glass candle holder off the nightstand and threw it right at my head.

I ducked. "What the fuck?!" I yelled. "What's wrong with you?!" I walked over to her before she could grab anything else.

"What's wrong with me?! What's wrong with me?!" She broke down crying in my arms. "Why don't we ask your pregnant bitch what's wrong with me?! I can't believe I trusted you!" She cried so hard; her body shook.

I scooped her up into my arms and laid her on the bed. Then, I kicked my shoes off and got in with her. "I know I fucked up. I'm sorry, ma. I didn't mean for it to happen. I swear I didn't...but ma, you gotta calm down. For the baby."

She turned her back toward me and cried harder. "Just leave."

"I'm not going anywhere and you not either. I'm sorry and I'll make it up to you." I put my arm around her and rubbed her belly.

"How?!" She questioned then choked a little on her tears.

"I don't know...but I am." I kissed the back of her neck.

She continued to cry; so, I continued to hold her. I woke up to a loud scream about an hour later.

"Oh my God!!! No!!!" She cried out in a tone I had never heard her voice reach before.

I jumped up out of my sleep. "What's wrong?!" I opened my eyes to find her hands covered in blood. I pulled away from her a little and saw it was all on the front of my jeans and back of her shorts too. I hopped out of bed and called 911.

Surprisingly, they came within ten minutes. They strapped her to the gurney and rolled her out to the ambulance. As I tried to get in behind her, she stopped me. "Don't bring yo ass in here! This shit is all your fault! Just stay the fuck away from me!" The paramedic closed the door, locking me out but I could still hear her screaming. "Fuck you, Rick! Don't come to that fucking hospital!"

I hopped in my car and followed behind them. They rolled her out and she immediately started to scream again when she saw me. "I hate you! You a dirty dick, nasty muthafucka! I hate you! I swear I hate yo ass!" I kept quiet and followed behind her bed.

That shit was a year ago. She lost our baby that day and I almost lost her. I don't know why, but that briefly crossed my mind as Tameka climbed to rest her knees on each side of my head.

I closed my eyes and ran my tongue from her clit to her pussy hole. I dipped my tongue in and out a few times. Then I licked back up to her clit. Flicking the tip of my tongue against her clit, I slapped her ass.

"Make it cum." She demanded and rocked her hips in the direction she wanted my tongue to slide.

Twenty minutes later, I had her folded up. Head on the bed, ass in the air and legs hanging over her face. I felt her body tense and sucked her clit sloppily. When I let her go, she was out of breath. "Make it cum again."

"Woman, you came five times already."

"Is RJ spending the night?"

I shook my head. "Yes."

"I want... to cum... again." She hissed.

"You wrong for that."

"I may be wrong for this but you were wrong for that. Eating a little more pussy should be a small thing to a giant."

I sucked her pussy with my mind racing. As soon as she came, I got up.

She stared up at me. "Where you going?"

I smiled. "I just finished eating your pussy. I'll be back with RJ after I finish eating hers."

Keno Said It...

Competition

Let me break this down for you. Say you know you have the best Mac and Cheese dish in your family. You meet your now husband; but whenever at a table with his mom's Mac and Cheese and yours, he always chooses his mother's. So, one day, you ask him in a joking manner, "Like, what the fuck? You like your mom shit better than mine?" He says, "Her shit be having that drip... that extra cheesy type shit. They're both good; I just like the different cheese flavors she puts in."

Boom! Now you're in the kitchen one Sunday, fucking up this family recipe you been slaying every Thanksgiving with for the last fifteen years all because without realizing it, you have put yourself in competition. This is no different than when you're in a relationship. It may be with someone you don't even care to keep anymore; but the minute you find out someone else has that person's attention, you're like, *hold the fuck up.* Your subconscious kicks into competition mode. *This motherfucker must have forgotten who I am.* Now you're doing shit you used to do, like more oral, sexier clothing, calling more, texting more; even doing shit you have never done. It may be opening yourself up to threesomes, going to strip clubs or whatever it takes to please this partner you didn't even want just two months ago. Yes, competition will have you on your heals; but some competition is healthy and some is not. So, make your next move your best move.

"I guess ignorance is bliss, because I don't want to know."

-A woman who definitely knows he's cheating.

What They Don't Know

"What they don't know won't hurt me." I mean that respectfully, disrespectfully... however a muthafucka take it. I'm dealing with some real shit in my life...but who not? I'm not obligated to tell a female my business and it ain't lying if she don't ask me specifically. I don't feel bad about the situation with Alliyah. It is what is it. I mean, it's a life lesson for her.

She told me the day we met; she had been looking for a job for weeks. She had gotten emotional and quit her previous job without thinking. Clearly, she did a lot of shit like that... without thinking. Anyway. The day we met she was going on an interview at a job she wanted so badly. She said she waited forever to get that call to work as a receptionist at high-end magazine (I won't say which one to protect the innocent); so, her mind was all over the place on the way there.

I was riding a bike, which I did some days when the urge hit me. She ran into me...literally. She hit me with her car, knocking me into the street. I got a few bumps and bruises. "What the fuck?! Don't tell me you didn't see me." I immediately started yelling.

She got out looking like she might cry. "I am so sorry." She covered her mouth. "Oh my God. Are you okay?"

I stared at her as she let her eyes roam all over me, stopping briefly at my arms and shoulders. I held in the smile that threatened the seriousness of the situation. "Yeah. I'm good; but you gotta do better." I dusted myself off.

A car rode past us and a woman yelled out of her window. "Call the cops!"

Another woman walking past stopped to say, "Hell yea! Call the fucking police!"

Some dude pulled out his phone. "Unun. I'm calling them."

I let her get an eyeful if my six-foot three frame. I even ran my hand over my bald head to draw her attention to it.

By then, she was frantic. "Listen, my license is suspended because of some old tickets I haven't had the money to pay." I could see fear takeover her.

Looking down at my bike, I got pissed all over again...but I managed to calm myself. "Calm down, I'm fine. You do owe me for the bike; but no one's going to jail today." I assured her. "I'm Wilson; what's your name?"

She flashed a weak smile. "I'm Alliyah."

Finally getting a good look at her, I realized this woman was beautiful. Big hazel eyes, long dark curly hair, full lips and although she was slim... her small ass was still poking. "I'll tell you what..." I started. "You treat me to dinner and we'll forget about the whole thing."

She squinted her eyes like she was considering my offer. A policeman pulled up and helped her make up her mind. "Sure, we can do that. It's just dinner, right?"

"Right." I agreed.

The officer walked over to where we were standing. "I got a call about an accident."

"Yes, officer." I took the lead. "But no one here is hurt; and we have worked compensation for the damages out amongst ourselves."

The officer looked from me to her. "Is that true, miss?"

She nodded. "Yes. We have everything worked out. Thank you for coming so fast."

He looked down at my bike and back at me. "Okay. Well, I hope you both do the right thing in your agreement." With that, he walked back to his car and sat for a few minutes. Then he pulled off slowly.

We exchanged numbers but neither of us called. It wasn't until a week later that she crossed my mind. I had just gotten the worse head I had ever received from anyone. Then, I watched this woman stomp around my condo gathering her things.

"I shouldn't have sucked your little ass dick anyway. Yo ungrateful ass don't deserve it." She hissed.

"Can't be too little. As big as your mouth is, I still ended up getting scraped by your teeth." I laughed.

"Fuck you! No, I regret doing that already!" She stormed out, slamming my front door behind her.

"Give it some time, sweetie. You'll find out just how much more you'll regret it." I mumbled to myself because I knew damn well she could no longer hear me.

I walked into my kitchen and grabbed a bottle of water. As I chugged it down, my eyes landed on my bike-which I still hadn't replaced. The bent front tire made me think of her. So, I searched my contacts for her number.

She answered on the first ring. "I know. I know. I should have called you; but if you give me a little more time, I can replace your bike." She said right away.

"Okay...but I was calling about that dinner you owe me. I was thinking tonight would be a good night to cash in on that."

"Ummm. Okay. Tonight.... will be fine; where did you have in mind?"

"I'll text you the address. Let's say... seven. If dinner goes well, we can just forget about the bike like I told you that day. " I replied.

"Cool. See you then." I could hear the relief in her voice.

"Yes, see you then." I returned.

She ended our call with a nervous, "Okay, bye."

Satisfied with myself, I made a few business calls and got showered to go home to my soon-to-be ex-wife.

We argued as usual. There was nothing we could agree on lately. The marriage was dead and I couldn't understand for the life of me why her ass was holding on. It was getting harder and harder not to tell her, especially with all the shit she popped.

Since she started the argument, I didn't need an excuse to leave. I just got dressed and walked out the door. Her stubbornness kept her from asking me anything.

Instead of texting Alliyah the address to the restaurant, I asked her for hers and sent a car to pick her up. My driver was used to making the kind of first impression I was going for. Still, I had him pick her up in the Tesla.

I called to let her know to come out and I could hear the surprise all in her voice. I still hate that I didn't get to see the look on her face.

"A Tesla?! You sent a Tesla to pick me up? This must have costed you a fortune." She whispered.

I laughed. "Get in. I'll see you there." I hung up smiling ear to ear.

Dinner was more pleasant than I expected. Her conversation was interesting...far from the usual small talk I was anticipating having to sit through. We talked about some of the places I've traveled to and some she would like to visit. We discussed a small business idea she had been sitting on for what she knew to be way too long. She even selected a great wine choice.

We laughed and flirted and talked for almost four hours. Then she sighed and thanked me for letting her off the hook for the accident.

I sent her home in the same car. My driver told me that half way to her house, she surprised him.

"I feel bad. This is such a nice car and you've been so nice. I wish I had a tip for you."

He appreciated the thought. Maybe it even caught him off guard because he said, "Mr. Wilson pays me well. I don't need a tip. He's a great boss."

I know she must have been so confused because with all the talking we did... my affluence never came up.

He filled her in because I had neglected to tell him not to. "You didn't know that this was his car you're riding in? Or his restaurant you ate at?"

She sank into the back seat and road quietly the rest of the way. She texted me that night and that was the beginning of us dating.

I took her on trips, helicopter rides, and private dinners on rooftops. After a while, we were together more than we were apart and things we going better than even I could have planned. We only slowed down because she was working more hours at the magazine.

Because of all the extra effort she was putting in at work, her boss had also become intrigued by her. She had not only done the job of being the receptionist, she had managed to come up with an ad idea and headline for that month's top story. She was quickly making a name for herself around the office.

It wasn't long before her boss had realized how motivated, sweet, and smart she was and pulled her from behind the desk. She got Alliyah booked for a few modeling gigs and the offers came pouring in.

Ten months in, she was calling me "daddy" on an almost nightly basis; and her boss (who she called Z) had become a professional mentor and somewhat a mother to her. Sometimes they seemed even closer- like best friends. My lack of interest in my wife's dealings and happenings and tunnel vision when it came to Alliyah's body and sex drive had me completely in the dark about how close to home the situation really was.

This is when all my secrets and sins got put center stage. One day, she walked into Z's office and found her crying. Z told her she had just found out she was sick. When she explained how sick, they cried together. Z got so upset just talking about our situation that she took a picture of us from her desk drawer and threw it against the door.

Alliyah caught a glimpse and asked the obvious. "Is this Wilson? How do you know him?"

Z sniffled. "Wilson? Wilson is my dead brother-in-law. That is my cheating, lying husband Donte. He is how I got HIV."

Alliyah choked on her words. "This. Is. Your- your husband?" She sat down holding her stomach.

Z squinted her eyes. "Yes. Why?"

"Z, I have to tell you something. I swear I didn't know." She grabbed her boss's hand. She told her everything from how we met to the address of the condo she slept with me in.

Of course, she called me crying and screaming and so did Zamaiyah. It wasn't the first time I had slept with one of her employees so that had no effect on my decisions whatsoever. It was Zamaiyah taking her under her professional wing that sent everything into a tail spin. I didn't have shit to explain to either of them. Don't get me wrong, Alliyah was the best pussy I've had in a minute and I'll miss her...but I don't owe her shit. As far as Z is concerned...her ass is still around. The majority of the money is mine. Where is she gonna go? Especially with what I gave her. That bitch is mine for life. Alliyah could have kept enjoying the money too if she was smart. What can I say? Bitches just don't think anymore.

Keno Said It...

Everything That Glitters....

It's okay to want a person and never actually experience them. Nowadays, people get off on instant gratification and end up struggling to deal with the consequences. Sometimes, that man or woman isn't even who or how you think they are. Often, lifestyles that look too good to be true aren't true at all. You take on risks of all sizes when make a habit of leaping before you look and see where you might land yourself. Yes, the decisions of your life are all yours to make; but if you insist on being a daredevil, learn to live with the injuries.

"Half of these muthafuckas if fuckin' they homies anyway?"

-A woman that will still lay down for him.

D.L Dilemma

I leaned my back against the wall as she bounced her fat ass back. My face was still wet from licking all on her chocolate-colored flesh, but I thought I might want another taste for the road as I enjoyed the view. We had been sneaking off for these little sessions for the last six months. Couldn't get more than ten minutes at a time; but you'd be surprised what you can get accomplished in that little time when you put your mind to it. I felt her pussy walls tighten around me and knew she was cumming. She reached back and ran her fake fingernails on my stomach. "Cum with me." She moaned.

Four minutes later, I was back in my cell washing the evidence off. Flashes of the sad look on her face as she kissed me for what we both knew would be the last time danced around in my head. I learned years back not to get emotionally attached; but she had definitely been my favorite pastime. I smiled to myself at the thought while I packed what I wanted to take with me.

"Grand! Let's go!" Another guard called my name and I couldn't get out of my cell fast enough. I glanced back briefly. "Take care of yourself, man." I told my celly, then walked out without waiting for his response.

The walk from the block I had called home to the front gate seemed like the longest walk I had ever taken. It felt like a weight was lifted off my chest when that first burst of fresh air hit my face.

It was only 56 degrees out and windy too; but nobody could tell me it didn't feel like the first of summer.

"See you in a few months." The guard said with a chuckle; but I didn't get the joke.

I shot her a side-glance, then refocused on the parking lot I was stepping into. No one was there to pick me up; I didn't have anyone waiting to take me home. It wasn't that people wouldn't be happy to see me free; but the hard lesson I... and every other man in that prison... had to learn is that life goes on without you.

I thought about how I would get home, but my feet just kept going. Before I knew it, they had taken me two miles away. I walked into a BP gas station and asked the clerk, "Hey, can you call me a cab?"

He looked at me like I was speaking Martian. "A cab?" He was a young kid. Maybe 18, 19 or 20.

"Yeah. Do you have a number for one?" I pressed.

He laughed. "No."

A woman walked up behind me. "Just got out?"

I turned to face her. "Is it that obvious?"

"Yes. Nobody takes cabs anymore." She smiled and a single dimple appeared. "Where you going? I'll call you a Lyft."

"A Lyft?" I frowned. "What the fuck is that?"

The clerk laughed and I shot him a glance that stopped his ass mid-giggle.

She cleared her throat but I knew she was cutting off a laugh of her own. "It's like a new version of cabs."

I leaned in to watch what she was doing over her shoulder. She jerked her head around to look me in the eyes first; but when I matched her gaze, she calmly turned her attention back to her phone. I watched her doing it, but still couldn't believe things had changed so much.

"See?" She angled her phone so I could get a good look. "It'll be here in six minutes." I'll wait until it pulls up so you don't miss it."

I let my eyes roam from her phone to her hand and up her arm. Her petite but curvy frame made her just the type of woman I would have pursued before I went in.

"Excuse me." She called to me.

"Yes, you have to forgive me. You're a very beautiful woman." I pardoned myself.

"Thank you." She blushed. Then she caught herself. "Well, I'm going to pay for my drinks, then go out to my car. It's not cold or anything so you'll be fine waiting. Nothing against you... I just don't know you like that."

I nodded. "Understood." I peeled a bill off the money I had been given back from the day I got arrested; $975. I had over five grand but the arresting officer must have helped himself. "Let me get that for you." I paid the clerk and walked out.

The car came and after thanking her, I got in. She came to the window. "Have a good first day home."

"Thank you." I smiled.

She walked away and the car pulled off. I got to my destination and went on with my plans, thinking I would never see her again.

A month later, I was back on my feet. I had called in a few favors some people owed me from back in the day and got back on my feet on no time. I had made a name for myself before I went in and standing on that was my only option. It wasn't that I hadn't thought about living a different life; I had thought about that a lot in that ten years I was lock up. It just wasn't possible for me. I had to play the cards I had been dealt. So, I played like a spades champ.

I was at that same gas station one day, my mind on so many other things. I was zoned out when she walked up to car.

"I see it didn't take you long to bounce back." She said with a smile.

I looked up and the sun had her glowing. I smiled back. "How you doing, good Samaritan?"

"Lucky for you." She shot back.

"True. You should let me repay you." I took the opportunity to shoot my shot.

"How you plan on doing that?" She raised an eyebrow.

"Let me take you out." I offered.

She thought about it, all the while looking into my eyes like she could read me if she stared hard enough. After a minute, she finally said, "Okay."

"Give me your number. I'll text you and let you know what time I'm picking you up." I handed her my phone.

"Sounds like a plan." She said as she handed my phone back to me.

I picked her up at eight o'clock that night. She came out in a tight-fitting tan dress and heels. I remember noticing her white painted toes. The date was just the beginning. We ate and talked and everything was going great. I mean, I was really enjoying myself. Then she laughed and it was all over for me.

I knew right then I was keeping her; and apparently, she felt the same because she had no shame about taking me back to her house afterwards. That pussy was good too. It was so wet and tight; I stayed in that muthafucka all night.

The next morning, she woke me up with her mouth. She sucked on the head of my dick like it was a pacifier. When I woke up squirming, she slowly let the full length of my dick slide to the back of her throat. She sucked me in and out of her mouth, letting her spit drip down around it. Then she made slurping sounds as she came back to the tip. I was in heaven. When I finally came, she drank up every drop. That was a year ago.

This woman turned out to be everything I wanted. She wasn't only beautiful, but she was smart and she brought me peace. She was understanding and fun loving. She was literally exactly how I would describe the perfect woman and coming home to her and her son was actually something I looked forward to every night.

We moved in with each other a week ago and surprisingly it was barely an adjustment. It was like we just fit. So, I never expected what came next. I didn't even have a chance to really enjoy what family life was like.

Seven days. For seven days, I had everything I wanted. Then on the eighth day, her son was looking in the boxes in the garage. If I had known, I would have asked him what he was looking for and found it myself.

I knew he had seen them right away because I could hear his reaction loud and clear. "Ewe, that's nasty! Ma!"

I ran into the garage before her but not fast enough to get them tucked before she walked in.

Her eyes got wide as she spotted them. "What the fuck?!" She jerked her head in my direction.

I couldn't form words to even begin to explain myself.

"How? You fuck me every night. You went to prison for murder. What the fuck is that?" She pointed at one of the photos.

Again, I was speechless. I never thought it would come out.

"Hello! Yo down-low ass better say something! Shit, now that I think about it, prison is probably where these shits were taken." She picked up a couple of the pictures and held them up for me -and her son- to see.

One was a picture of my old cellmate sitting on my lap. In another, we were kissing. In a third, he was laying on my chest in my bunk. To be honest, seeing them almost made me smile. It was the last time I was able to fully be myself.

"Your gay ass don't have anything to say? Don't you think you owe me at least an explanation as why you didn't tell me?" Her frustration quickly became anger. "You know what? Don't say shit, just get your shit out my house and leave. Now!"

"Okay." It was all I offered before turning to walk away.

She beat my back with her fists. "You faggot son of a bitch! Go back to that boy pussy you like!"

I turned around so fast, she flinched back like she thought I would hit her. Instead, I calmly told her, "I will. It's way tighter than that loose shit you been giving me." It was only half true.

It hurt to walk away, but I knew the bitch would never see me the same.

Keno Said It...

What's makes her sex good?

Is it the wetness? Is that why the rumors of pregnant "jay jay" seem so real? Is it the tightness? I mean, when it's wrapped around a man's nature, is it enough to make a man sing to his momma about you? Or is it the activity you put in? The pushing back and forth, the taking control, going from your back to doggy style, climbing on top, the loud moans? Is it a combination of all of the above?

Let me answer this for you. It may be a combination of them all; but for sure, on a very large percentage, a man has to be feeling you. That's what brings him back time after time. Majority of the time, he doesn't even realize it. It's not the sex only that makes him want the sex? It's you! It's that something about you, that clicks in your meet ups, those certain mannerisms or behaviors, the sexiness.

Now here's the irony, that one thing that will confuse the shit out of you. The one thing that makes men so hard to figure the fuck out. This is big… okay, are you ready? For some men, it's the way you submit to him, and how thoughtful you can be. I mean, those calls during the morning saying "Stop by, I made you lunch" and "I just got out the shower, come see me." Oh, that shit drives some men up the wall! Shit like when he touches you and you're already on go. That chemistry is a two-way street; when his touch or voice makes you quiver and get moist. Yeah, you're feeling him just as much as he's feeling you…but now here goes the part that makes you say men are from fucking Mars. Some men… no matter how many ways you try to please them, no matter how much you cook and clean, they will be out there looking for that two-dollar beer drinking pussy or that Red Bottom, Gucci bag toting broad. This is because the level of the female doesn't attract all men. Sometimes, his attraction is the fact you're not chasing him, his low level of access to you, your stubbornness, the hard to get, the late returns on texts, not praising him the way these other females do.

I know this is a catch 22, don't kill me. I didn't write the playbook! Yes, us men can be bitchy too, downright hard to figure out at times. That's why it's important to keep a good one when you find them. They are scarce, but some still do exist; and most of all, don't change up on a man or for a man. What attracts him is what attracts him.

"What's good for the goose is good for the gander."

-A woman who will cheat back.

<u>What Goes Around...</u>

People talk about love like there's only one way to do the shit right. One man, one woman. One way to show that you love that one person. I'm a walking example of how you can't control love... no matter how bad you want to.

I fell in love with Deja when she was 16 years old; I was 20. If that wasn't problematic enough, I was already in a relationship with my son's mother. Before you judge me, understand that I wasn't planning to love anybody outside of my relationship. I mean, I'm a man so yeah...I fucked around but I never got attached. Deja was just different.

Out of nowhere, her friend handed me a four-page love letter and said Deja wrote it to me. I ducked off and read it. I had to sit with what is said for a minute... especially the last paragraph.

"... In your eyes, I see passion personified. Love as a living, breathing drug I look forward to becoming addicted to. You stir my soul with just a glance. I know I'm not supposed to think about you this way but thoughts of you make my whole-body blush and I had to fill you in or I'd be doing myself a major injustice. I owe it to my body... to my heart...to let you have me; even if it's just for a short while. Think about it because it's all I can think about..."

52

I knew I should have crumbled her little love note and acted like her young ass was invisible to me; but her words... her mind had struck a chord with me. I had to see what she was about. In hindsight, I fully understand why other people judged me. I probably would have looked at another dude my age fucking with her sideways too; but I wouldn't do a got damned thing differently. Deja is the love of my life.

Her body was perfect. She tasted just as good as she felt and her sex was...well I'll just say I was addicted.

One night, I couldn't get much time away. So, I picked her up and parked on a dead-end street. She climbed into my lap and her pussy was wet without me even touching her. Had me feeling like the pussy loved me too. She slid down on my dick and put her feet on either side of me. Then she slowly rode me. We kissed as she slid up and down my shit like I was her personal amusement park ride. Then she put my seat back and rode my face while she sucked all of her wetness off of me. When I came, she swallowed every drop. We stayed on that dead-end for three hours, making each other cum over and over again. We had so many nights like that...when we couldn't get enough of each other and she let me have her however, whenever, wherever. *Who was gonna compete with that?*

I was fucking with this girl for 20 years. In that time, we have never actually committed to being in a relationship. We both just knew what it was. It was the women I ended up in relationships with that needed help coming to the understanding.

Lena was the first I had to sit down and she took it hard. "What the you mean, you love her?! Who the fuck is this bitch?!"

"When you do find that out, I'm telling you now. Don't lay a hand on her. Not a muthafucka finger." I warned her because Lena liked to fight.

"Or what, Devin? You gonna fight me? Over the next bitch? What type of time you on?" She said with tears welling in the corners of her eyes.

"Find out." It was all I offered her. I didn't want to hit her, but I had before and if it came to that... I would again.

"Are you fucking serious, Devin?" Her voice cracked as she lost the fight she had been waging with her tears and they came streaming down her cheeks. Lena had never looked as beautiful to me as she did in that moment but maybe I say that because it ended up being one of our last civil moments together.

I ended up having to put hands on her multiple times. Then one day she up and left. I can't say I blame her. Deja had been taking up most of my nights and some of my days too. Any time I could get away, we would disappear together. She didn't ask me for anything other than time alone and I never had that in a woman. Doing what I did, women had a habit of finding shit to need. Deja was a breath of fresh air...a peaceful spot in a world where all we knew was how to make noise. It's fucked up to say but when Lena left, I didn't give a fuck. As long as I still had access to my son.

After Lena, Deja went down south with her mother. She never said why, but I still think she might have been pregnant when she left. Either way, while she was gone, I met Keri.

Keri was my hood bitch. She ran packs for me when I needed her to, she was with me when I "worked", kept work at her spot. She played her position-which was all the shit I would never allow Deja to do.

Deja was innocent, a for lack of better words. Yeah, she was fucking me but she didn't smoke or drink or hang out. Seemed like I was her only bad decision a lot of the time. When she came back, we picked up like she never left.

Eventually, Keri found out about Deja and I had to sit her down too. She surprised me when she responded, "I can tell you love her...and I found some of the poems she wrote you. I know she loves you too." She cried; but she hung around a lot longer than Lena did.

I found out later that she ended up calling and eventually approaching Deja. The fucked-up part about it was that she didn't want to fight her. She wanted to find out for herself what it was about this girl that I couldn't leave alone. I wasn't for none of that shit. Maybe another nigga would have wanted to have them both at once; but I wasn't sharing Deja.

One day, Keri came to me. "I'm asking you to stop fucking with her."

"I told you. I'm never leaving her. She gonna have to stop fucking with me." The words came out effortlessly and I meant every one.

"So, you don't care if it hurts me?" She looked me square in the eyes.

I don't think I even blinked. "No. I don't. Make your decision; stay and deal with it or don't. Like I said though...I'm not gonna stop fucking with Deja. I love her."

"I thought you loved me." She started to cry.

"I do, but that don't have shit to do with Deja and vice versa." I explained, somewhat losing my patience.

"I'm pregnant, Devin." She told me.

"Okay. What you wanna do about it?" I asked, fine with whatever she decided.

"What am I gonna do?" She walked off crying. "Fuck you, Devin!"

She had an abortion but we stayed together. Meanwhile, I was still fucking Deja faithfully. Still, because she had a habit of pulling Houdini tricks, I worried I would see her one day and she might be gone the next. So, I came inside her on purpose and often. I wanted her forever.

If Deja ever got pregnant by me, she never kept it- and I tried so many times. She never said a word about it either. She just disappeared on me one day. When I saw her two years later, she had a baby that she said was by some other nigga I never heard of. The shit crushed me but I let it go to have her back in my life. Besides, Keri had given me a son.

Finding out I was back fucking Deja sent Keri over the edge. She started fucking around too. Had a bitch and a nigga just trying to make me jealous. I just cut the bitch off. She had spent and taken and lost too much of my money anyway.

Deja left me again. No explanation, no goodbye. When I saw her again, she was married to a whole different muthafucka. I couldn't understand it. She even gave the nigga a baby.

I took that shit on the chin because she was still willing to lay down for me but deep down, I wondered why she wouldn't fuck with me on that level.

By that time, I had a third son with Arielle. She and I never were together. She just locked up on one of my drunk nights. Still, I had to sit her ass down too. She needed to know who Deja was to me.

"Fuck you and fuck that bitch. Just make sure you have my money when I need it." The money hungry bitch gave me the perfect response. I never wanted to bring any problems to Deja.

I loved her in a way I couldn't even tell her until two nights ago. We were laying in a hotel room. Fully dressed, just talking. She had disappeared on me again. So, this time I had to pour my soul out to her.

"I tried for years to get you pregnant. I was hoping like hell you came to me one day and said your son was mine. Or even your daughter. All the times you left, I wondered why you never asked me to go with you?"

Before she could respond, there was a banging on the door. I peeked through the peephole and confirmed what I already knew. My live-in girlfriend, Tracy had caught me. I let her in and to our surprise. She sat down calmly. "With her?" She looked from me to Deja.

"I told you about this. It is what it is. I love her." I said nonchalantly.

She frowned. "That's it? After all our plans and you telling me you will never hurt me just hours ago? It just is what it is?"

"Yeah." I took Deja's hand and caressed it. I wanted her to know I wouldn't let shit happen to her. She shook her head in shock.

"So, it's just fuck my feelings?!" Tracy pressed.

"We have it figured out. Y'all other muthafuckas have shit to figure out. Not me ...not us." I put my arm around Deja's waist and pulled her close to me.

"Fuck you. I hope that bitch got a place for you to stay." Tracy stormed out of the room.

I turned to Deja. "I'm sorry."

"Don't apologize to me. That's your woman. You need to go apologize to her." She said softly.

"No. You're my woman."

"To be honest...In the beginning, I had five niggas at once. I was young and living my life. I mean, I loved you...I still do but you always had somebody. And really, when I got older, I came to understand that if you were willing to cheat on everybody with me...I'd be stupid to believe you wouldn't cheat on me. That's why I would never agree to a relationship." Her words flowed like velvet because her voice and tone were so sweet; but they still cut me.

"Would never or will never?"

"Both. I'm sorry but you need to go home and apologize to that woman. You owe her at least that. Be a better person than that." She had the audacity to say.

I couldn't say shit. I just stared into her pretty brown eyes.

"She took your car keys. Ima put you in a Lyft. Go talk to her."

I walked out thinking, *ain't this a bitch*. I apologized to Tracy and we're still together but I miss Deja's little soft-hearted ass like an addict misses their drug of choice.

I think about the shit sometimes, like I am now. Kicking myself in the ass every time I think about the fool I was. Then I thank God Tracy accepted my apology. We got married and had twin girls. We bought a house together just like we had planned; but don't get me wrong it wasn't a "happily ever after" situation.

Just when I thought things couldn't have been anymore perfect, somebody snitched about the cocaine I was running and we took a raid. Yeah, I said "we" because she wore the weight and took two years so I wouldn't go to jail.

I sent money every week along with pictures of the kids and I visited twice a month because those were the only days that I could get away. Deja would stay over on Fridays because her boyfriend was a trucker that traveled. So, on Fridays she would stay over and keep the kids Saturday morning while I went to the visit.

Yeah, I know it's fucked up, and I know six to seven of you gullible motherfuckers been in Tracey's shoes. Fighting for love, hoping to win a man to yourself one day. Again, don't get me wrong. There's nothing wrong with fighting for what and who you love; but if the person you're pursuing has clearly given you every sign... on top of honestly stating their true desires and plans, why would you expect different reactions from the same play book? That's what they call insanity; but in the real world we call it love...

Keno Said It...

Bill Payer or Bullshitter?

Some men are real bill payers and some are real bullshitters. It's your job to learn to recognize who is who. You know a man when you see him. I mean, that motherfucker that knocks you off your feet. That motherfucker who you can tell his momma raised him right or that he watched his dad hold it the fuck down. He's selfless; house before bullshit. Bills may not be covered exactly on time all the time, but they are priority in his book. He refuses to do goofy shit before his lady and kids are comfortable, he actually leaves the check - sometimes on the table. He's not hiding bank statements, raises, lottery winnings, shit like that. He's texting you: **Babe, are we caught up with everything?** Before he walks in the door, he hits the phone like: **you need anything from the grocery store**, or **did you cook, if not I'll grab us something. I know you're probably tired with them kids running you raggedy all day**. See these types of men are genuine for the most part. I'm not saying they have to have a bunch of money to throw around. I'm saying what they do have, they know home satisfaction comes first. This is the man you should learn to bend or flex for. The man you should be working to better communicate with, the one who's "swag" you need to be trying to match.

Then, you have the bullshitter. The motherfucker that will take the bills out the mailbox and bring them right to your gullible ass. Yes, gullible is one of my favorite words to get my point across when describing females like this. No offense, but it's direct. Now back to what I was saying about this bullshitting ass momma's boy. This is usually a selfish wannabe Muslim on Christmas, but accepting watches from you on his birthday ass ninja. No disrespect to the men of faith at all; I'm talking about the ones pretending for their own gain. I'm talking about the good Christian and or the Atheist, I'm talking about the motherfucker who pick fights when bills are due. The motherfucker who got the nerve on a Friday to stop by the block, after he cashes that $400 dollar check and buys motherfuckers drinks like he hit the lottery, smoking an eighth of weed and pack of cigs. Then walks in the door with $180, talking about he needs to buy himself the new Jordan's. The ninja that hits a scratch off or lottery ticket and hides the shit in a small pocket in his wallet. The brother that sells dreams. Mr. "that shit crazy", who shakes his head when you tell him the electric bill is $800 dollars, but he got that bullshit Gucci belt last week with his Tommy underwear and wife-beata tucked inside. I'm talking about the weirdo that thinks only covering the 120 dollars of your end of Section 8 is holding his house down. The motherfucker that only leaves the car in the driveway when it's out of gas or touching on "E". The ninja that takes the whole income tax and buys a bullshit car with no license or insurance knowing the kids need spring and summer clothes. Wait, hold up… am I saying too much? Do you know this guy? Is he the one you call zzzaddy? The one that will eat the last of the kid's cereal on a school morning. The one that will wait to get to work to take a shit because you're out of toilet paper or will hold his shit until you buy some tissue. The bullshitter will come home knowing there's no tissue and sit his inconsiderate ass on the bowl. Then open the door up with his funky ass and ask you, "ain't no type of tissue out there? No napkins or nothing?" I'm talking about the ninja you keep giving your money to flip, but he keeps buying weed packages and smoking the shit up with his broke ass homeboy. Then, when he's high, he slings some good dick so you're willing to take the loss. "It's just a minor setback", as he would phrase it. I'm taking about Mr. "killer" that does all the yelling in the house like he's king but no providing. The one who stands on the block all day long and returns with less than what he had. I remember hearing the phrase, "you must be out there selling the money". I almost spit my juice in my coworker's face, while she was describing her fiancé. She was on a roll. She said the negro always yelling he on a money chase but she wants to ask him so bad how fast do the money be running. You can't make this shit up.

This type of man may eventually grow… but sis, not right now. Maybe no time soon. You have kids, let him go back to his momma and let her finish where she left off. That's not your responsibility unless you just love being a gullible ass chick. Okay, I'm retiring it now. Gullible is dead… just like that relationship …

"You need to show me the proper respect!"
-A woman who doesn't know how to earn her place.

<u>*Musical Chairs*</u>

Women are always complaining that us men are immature. Some men are; but there are a lot of situations where the women are the fucking problem. What the fuck is the beef between our women and our mothers? The shit is silly. I would know, I been in the middle of that goofy ass shit for a while now. It all started one night after dinner one night.

I was rock hard after my shower. Thoughts of what I was about to do had danced around in my head all day. The anticipation had me throbbing as soon as I walked in the door.

As I slipped between the satin sheets, the smell of my after shower, Polo cologne filled the room. Dinner had been delicious; now it was time for dessert. Pressing my stone hard erection against my fiancée Angela's ass, I made his intentions clear. Usually, she would rock her hips gently, rubbing her round ass against my stiffness. This time, she didn't budge.

I thought to himself, *Oh, we're playing hard to get*. I was so used to her body submitting in response that this threw me off...but only briefly. I slid my hand up her thigh then around and up to cup her full breast in my hand and caress her nipple with my thumb. Still nothing.

"No response, hunh?" I knew what to try next. Maybe she was tired; but one thing she could never resist was the warmness of my moist tongue between her thick thighs. So, I proceeded to plan B. I started at her the back of her neck and kissed, licked and sucked my way down the side of her body. The smell and softness of her skin, drove me crazy. The more my mouth danced over her flesh, the harder my dick got. The first strike

64

of my tongue landed on target. Her body trembled but she still wasn't melting for me like usual.

Frustrated, I thought to myself, *fuck is this a leg locked like this for?* After kissing her hips to no avail, I asked with a bit of anger, "FUCK IS WRONG WITH YOU?"

Silence. Complete silence.

"Angela, you tripping! What's wrong? We just was good; ate a good ass dinner, danced; and came home to a clean house. What did I do in between to piss you off?"

She snatched away from me and sucked her teeth. "Okay, Everett. Like you don't fucking know."

I was clueless. "Angela, in the name of my savior Jesus Christ, I have no idea what are you talking about." The irony of my erection standing tall as I yelled "Jesus Christ" was awkward; but I had to make my point. I cut the light on. "Come on, Ang. I'm clueless."

"Everett, you don't think that was a little awkward?" She finally decided to say. "You telling me to let your mother sit in front while I'm already sitting there?"

She had to be fucking kidding me. "Ang, that's my mother. This is the way shit goes; this is the way we have always done. Why is it a problem all of a sudden?"

She sat up. "First off, I don't care what you've done with other bitches."

This bitch must have thought I was stupid. I wasn't about to lose my temper over some silly shit when that pussy was just about to heat up for me. "Ang, I meant we, as in you and I, we have done this before."

"Yeah, we have; but almost all of those times your father also in the back seat with her. That shit was mad weird...like we was the less important mother fuckers in the car."

"It's not like that, babe. You know that. After all this time, you gotta know that. Now come on, let me suck on you and fix this shit." I brought the conversation full circle.

She frowned. "Suck on me? You really think sex will fix this shit? Typical fucking man. If you wanna fix shit... you're about to be married, fix the fact that your mom obviously thinks you're her man."

The words "stupid bitch" burned the roof of my mouth but I wasn't going to let her make me take it there. "Wow, slow the fuck down. This conversation is getting out of hand when it's really not a big issue. I'ma speak to moms. Being honest, you do make some sense. I'm sorry if you felt disrespected."

I walked her back to the bed and her body responded to my tongue exactly how I was used to. It turned out to be a really good night.

Five months later: THE BABY SHOWER

We were half-way through the pregnancy but the gender was still a secret. I hoped for a baby boy; she prayed for a girl. The day came when we would finally know and someone's wishes would come true. My hands were sweating like crazy around the leather on my Range Rover steering wheel. The anticipation of my first child's gender was killing me.

I pulled up to my mother's front door to pick them up. Mom could usually look right at someone and tell what they were having. I was glad she had kept quiet about what she knew until the day came. Within minutes, my parents came out and unsurprisingly Mom walked right to the front passenger door. My heart fell through my asshole. I had totally forgotten about the last time we went through this. I never got to speak to Mom about it.

So, there could continue to be peace in my home, I had to do something. Shit was crazy; my wife sitting there, big as a house looking like she swallowed a watermelon seed; and my mom was shivering waiting for Angela to get out the front seat. I hopped out and said, "Hey, mom. You know with her being pregnant, sitting straight up may make her uncomfortable. I'll just help you get into the back."

My mother paused with a look of disbelief on her face. "You will do no such thing, Everett. You know I have a bad back."

"Mom, please..."

"Let your dad out. We'll catch a Lyft or Uber." She demanded.

"Mom!!" I couldn't believe these grown ass women were acting like this.

"To be honest, I'm not feeling so well. You can let your dad ride with you. I'm going to get some rest." It was the high-class equivalent of a toddler having a tantrum.

"Mom, it's my baby shower. My first baby." I wasn't about to just let her stay home because of a seat in the car.

"Everett I'm cold; I'm going back inside." She said and turned to walk away.

I leaned over to the passenger side. "Ang, you thi.... "

Angela cut me off. "Ain't no way in hell. Do yourself a favor and don't piss me off. I told you to handle this shit months ago." She was right...childish just like my mother; but I had told her I'd take care of it a while back.

67

I knew Mom wasn't budging, so I had to press her. "Ang, this is my mother."

With tears in her eyes, Angela said, "You're right. You're so, so, right." She opened the heavy Range door, stepped into the frigid air, and stood aside. "After you, queen." She slowly closed the door behind her mother-in-law before walking away crying.

I followed her. "Where are you going?" She didn't say a word. She didn't even look back. "Ang! Ang!" I yelled as I approached her. Grabbing her by her shoulders, I turned her around to face me.

With fire in her eyes, she hissed, "Don't touch me, motherfucker! And I mean it, Everett!"

Knowing how Ang can get when she's upset, I took my hands off her. I just watched as she pulled her phone from her purse. She made a call; the phone rang, then I heard her ask her brother to come pick her up. Our families only lived three blocks away from each other. That was how we met; we knew each other as kids. We stood there in silence. Me staring at her and her looking the other way.

Within minutes, her little brother pulled up to the curb. He hopped out. "What's up, E. Everything good?"

"Yeah, everything's okay. I'm sorry you have to be in the middle of this mess." I told him.

"It's cool, E. I was leaving out anyway; getting ready to go to the baby shower. So, it's all good." He assured me with a pat on my shoulder.

Angela rode off with her brother Marcus, tears running down her face and smearing the two hours of make-up she paid to have done.

The hall was beautiful. We had hired a catering company and party planners. Purple and silver were the colors. The DJ was playing R Kelly jams. I looked around and realized I had arrived before Angela. Family and friends filled the room and everyone seemed to be already enjoying themselves. Angela's mom was deceased, but all her other relatives came out to support.

Thirty minutes had passed; we were taking pictures, but still no Ang. I texted her maybe ten times apologizing and got not one response. I was calm on the outside but inside, I was going crazy. Ain't no way in the hell she wouldn't show up to her own baby shower... right? I had her cousin calling her and her brother but both were ignoring calls. So, I decided to head towards the car. Maybe go by her family's house. As I was heading out, two cops were coming in.

"Can I help you fellas?" I said in a calm tone.

The taller bald officer said, "Yes, are you familiar with an Angela and Kenneth Arlington?"

Already beginning to panic I replied, "Yes, that's my wife and brother-in-law. What's wrong? Why are you looking for them?"

"Sir, I'm not looking for them. I'm saddened to tell you she was in a bad car accident."

I fell to my knees as family members came to my aid.

The second officer added, "Sir, Kenneth didn't make it. He wasn't wearing a seat belt and we believe he was intoxicated. He was ejected through the windshield and was dead before he hit the ground."

The first interjected. "But your wife is okay... although she's hurt, she's alive. She's been rushed them to the University hospital."

Because of Covid, I was the only one allowed in the waiting room. I was lost, I blamed myself. I knew if I had put my foot down none of that shit would have been going on.

A doctor came up to me. "Hello, are you here for Ms. Arlington?"

"Yes, that's my wife. Is she okay? Doc, please tell me she's okay!" I pleaded.

"Yes, she's fine. We're operating." He informed me.

A lump formed in my throat. "Operating?"

"Yes, we're extracting the surviving twin. The boy, he's healthy and will be okay."

I couldn't help thinking that if she had just stayed in her place, we would be having both babies. *Who the fuck makes a nigga choose between them and their own mother?!*

Keno Said It...

Love and Lies

Ladies, that female intuition y'all love to say told y'all to go through your man's phone or personal items has to still work when he's talking to you. So many women have stories about how they were lied to by the men they loved and when I hear the lies, I think... she had to know he was lying. Infatuation will have you overlooking or turning the other cheek to the most obvious red flags and problems in a relationship. Don't confuse that with love. If you choose to ignore it when you know he's lying to you...is he really 100% at fault?

"You couldn't tell the truth to save your life."
-A woman who will know he's lying and is still goes along with it.

Liar, Liar

I don't think I've ever told a woman the whole truth. Maybe bits and pieces here and there; but never anything near the whole story. I've just never seen a situation where telling the entire truth would benefit me. Really, I don't even believe that type of situation exits. No woman alive can handle the whole truth and I learned that young.

Tasheena was the first girl I ever fucked and I had to lie just to get next to her ass.

"So, why I saw you walking Janise to her class yesterday, if I'm the one you want?"

"That's just my friend." I lied. Janise had already let me finger her but she said that was as far as she was willing to go. I had to move on. Respecting her and her choice to respect herself (somewhat) was played out. I needed a chick in the fast lane.

"So, you and her ain't kiss or nothing?" She frowned.

"Nah, Janise ain't like that." I told her.

"Well, I ain't either." She said. I guess we were lying to each other. I had already heard she was with the shits.

"You should come to my house after school." I took my shot.

She sucked her teeth. "How Ima get home? You ain't got no car."

"You can stay." That was the first true statement I had made the whole conversation. "I do what I want at my house. I don't know where my moms be most of the time... and she don't give a fuck what I do." Now that was a damn lie. Truth was, my mother worked two full-time jobs to keep us in that nice ass house; and if she had any idea I was sneaking that young hoe into her house, she would have killed me dead.

"So, I can stay the night with you?" She raised an eyebrow, just knowing I would say "no".

I smiled, knowing my mother wouldn't be home until well after we left for school at 7:45. "Hell yeah, if you want to. I mean, if you won't get in trouble for staying out." I called her bluff.

She stared me down for a minute.

"Well, what you gonna do? I gotta get back to class." I said, acting like her even standing in that hall talking to me wasn't the highlight of my boyhood to that point.

She sucked her teeth again and mumbled. "Nah, I ain't gonna get in trouble. My motha don't give a fuck about me either." She looked sad for a few seconds. Then tilted her head and smiled up at me. "I'ma meet you at the flag after last block. I can ride the bus home with you." She decided. "You better not leave me." She said before turning toward her class.

"I won't. Yo sexy ass gonna be mine tonight." I assured her.

Holding my excitement in was a struggle as I walked in the opposite direction to my class; but I wasn't going to risk the chance that anybody saw me get out of character. That night was going to be everything I had been waiting for since I found out what sex was.

She rode the bus home with me that afternoon, had the fellas whispering already. So, I knew I was going to be the man the next day.

74

When we got to my house, I tried to play it cool. Checked in with moms in a quick text then we sat and watched some TV. She snuggled under my arm with her head on my chest and I felt like the king of the castle. I couldn't wait to tell the boys about how she was on me. I made us some quick dinner plates from the leftovers moms had in the fridge for me. We sat across from each other and talked while we ate like we were on a real date. Damn near every other word that came out my mouth was a lie. She didn't know that though; she was looking into my eyes like my words were saving her life. Then we went up to my room. I had to lie to fuck her that night too.

"You did this before, right? I mean, you know what you doing, don't you?" She asked after I struggled to get her bra off.

"Yeah, I ain't no virgin." I lied through my teeth.

"Well, show me." She laid down on my bed and spread her legs. "Come kiss it."

Without hesitation, I pulled off my shirt and laid between her legs. I knew I had watched enough porn to fake it til I made it.

Shit, I lied my way into those panties for four weeks then broke up with her ass for the next best thing.

I lied to the next one too; and the next one and the next one. Like I said, I've lied to them all. The last one didn't even know my real name.

She never met any of my friends and damn sure not any of my family members. I told her that I worked 12 hour shifts six days a week. So, when I saw her, she didn't complain when all I wanted to do was stay in bed all day.

"You sleeping in again today, babe?" She asked me one day.

"Yeah, baby. I'm exhausted; but you know I'll sleep like a baby after you suck on this dick like a pacifier."

She actually laughed and laid between my legs ready to "put her baby to sleep". For six months that shit went on and I had it made.

Until one day, she hit me with a curve ball. I was damn near knee-deep in this big booty chick I had been lying to for six weeks. She finally let me in (both figuratively and literally).

"Oh my god! Don't stop! Rah, don't stop baby." She screamed as I tagged her ass doggy style like I was auditioning for my first roll in a porno. Rah, short for Rahmir, was yet another alias I was using.

I slapped her ass and it giggled like Jell-o. Right as I felt that first twinge of excitement indicating that I was close to cumming, I got an alert from Instagram saying: "Creshawna_too_bad mentioned you in her story" I couldn't fucking believe it. The bitch had pulled an honorable! I went to her story and there I was sleeping peaceful while she caressed me face and neck. The caption read: My Love.

My phone started going off like a slot machine on the winning spin.

Tanya: **Is this what the fuck we're doing now?!**

Celeste: **Oh you boo's tf up huh?!**

Angie: **My fucking friend?!**

Talece: **Fuck you!**

The texts kept coming. *Damn, this bitch had me fucked up.* I jumped out of bed and pulled on my clothes.

"What's wrong?! Where are you going?" She called after me but I was already headed out the door.

I hopped in my car right as my phone started ringing. I picked it up already expecting screams, but to my surprise the voice was calm.

"Look, I saw your little ghetto as love story. I ain't even mad because I knew you was for the streets. What you need to know is that I'm pregnant." I had never heard Celeste sound the way she did.

I didn't say a word.

"Good, so we on the same page about not wanting the muthafucka...I need half the money for this clinic." She added.

"How much?" I said as all the times she told me to pull out after I had already "shot up her club" ran through my head.

"Four fifty. Ima make the appointment." With that she hung up.

My phone rang again. I answered, "Yeah?"

"You think this shit is a game. You love playing with a muthafucka's feelings. Well, it's all good. I was fucking yo homeboy anyway." Tanya's voice hissed into my ear.

"So, what." I hung up. Somebody must have told that bitch wrong. I didn't give a fuck who else she was fucking.

My phone rang again. "Fuck!" I yelled, knowing my whole day would be like this. "Yeah."

Angie was already crying. "My friend? You had to be fucking my friend? Out of all the women in the city?" She sobbed loudly. "I fucking love you...dumb ass muthafucka! Don't you see that?"

"Angie, I told you I wasn't trying to get into a relationship. I told you I wasn't doing that love shit. You said you understood and was on the same page. What the fuck you thought changed?" I said, tired of dealing with feelings already.

"Okay. Come see me." She switched up just that fast.

I shook my head. "Aight, give me a few."

I drove straight to Creshawna's house. Her car was gone but I still took the steps and knocked on the door. After I was sure she wasn't home, I walked slowly back to my car checking my phone. Talece hadn't called or texted again. I guess it really was fuck me.

Ten minutes later, I pulled into a spot in front of Angie's building. I rushed upstairs because I had to take a piss.

She opened the door with puffy red eyes. "Angie, I didn't come here for-"

Out of nowhere something hit me in the back of my head so hard that everything went black. I woke up with a pounding headache. Squinting, I looked around trying to figure out what the hell had happened.

"Wake up, Darius." I heard Creshawna say and wondered what the fuck she was doing at Angie's.

"Darius? He told me his name was D'Andre." Angie barked. "You mean to tell me my ass was loving a nigga and I didn't even know his name?"

Creshawna laughed. "Shit, that's probably not his real fucking name either." She mushed my head. "He's such a fucking liar."

This is when I notice the switchblade she had in her hand. I tried to move and realized I was tied to the chair I was sitting in. I looked from Creshawna to Angie. Then back at Creshawna. "What the fuck are you crazy bitches gonna do?"

"Us crazy bitches are going to teach yo lying ass a lesson." Creshawna smiled devilishly. Then she leaned in and kissed my lips.

Angie's crazy ass saw that and pulled a small souvenir bat from behind her back. She swung it back behind her head and when it connected, it felt like my kneecap would come clean off.

I yelled at the top of my lungs. "AAHHHH!" I know somebody heard me.

"Aht, aht. We can't have that. Creshawna chuckled as she stuffed a scarf into my mouth.

I fought to push it back out, but she pushed it so far back that I began to choke.

Angie approached me, grabbed my jaw and kissed my lips too. All I could think was, *what the fuck*? I tried to talk. "Mmmm. Mmmm mmmhmhm."

"Oh, did you want to lie? I mean tell us something?" Creshawna tilted her head and the eerie look she gave me reminded me of a character from a horror movie.

"Mmmm!" I screamed.

"Yeah. He wants to lie to us some more, Cre." Angie agreed then slapped my face hard. "Shut your lying face. Did you really think you could just lie to us forever?"

I just stared her down. *What the fuck was I supposed to say if they could understand me?*

Creshawna came close with the knife and I moved and shuffled as much as I could; but she shoved the blade of that knife into my side like she was carving a steak. I felt a wave of heat wash over me then I felt weak. My eyes fluttered shut.

I woke up and this time, I was tied to Angie's bed and naked. Both of them came into the room wearing lingerie. My dick got hard immediately but I was trying my hardest to get it back down. I didn't want any part of whatever sick shit they were dealing with or planning.

"So, we talked about what the best outcome to this situation would be. Angie wants a baby. Now, why she would want a baby by yo trifflin ass is beyond me. I, on the other hand, know you're only good for one thing." She let her pointed acrylic fingernail graze my skin from my thigh all the way up my chest. Then she used it to lift my chin. "We talked and talked and came up with the only logical plan." She smiled at Angie who leaned in and kissed her lips.

My eyes got wide and they both laughed. Angie got onto the bed between my legs and started to give me head. I squirmed and tried to buck her off of me but my ankles were tied so tightly that all my struggling barely made a difference at all. She sucked on me so good that my body eventually gave in, despite my attempts against it. Before I knew it, I was moaning.

"That's right, baby." Creshawna purred. "Get into it." She played in Angie's hair and caressed her ass for a while.

Angie started moaning too and the feeling of the walls of her throat vibrating against the head of my dick drove me crazy.

80

I was moaning so loudly that it sounded like my voice was echoing around the room. Creshawna came back to kiss my lips. This time, I kissed her fine ass back.

She pulled away with a smile. Then climb to sit on my chest with her ass in my face. "Kiss this pussy just like that, okay?" She said over her shoulder.

Angie stopped sucking and eased her already wet pussy down onto my dick so she was sitting face-to-face with Creshawna. They started kissing and my dick throbbed with excitement. Creshawna arched her ass so that pussy was in my face and I licked all over that fat muthafucka.

She came on my tongue; Angie came on my dick and all the moaning they were doing made me shoot my load deep inside Angie just like she had been begging me to do every time we fucked.

They switched positions and I made sure they came again but as I was about to cum for the second time, Creshawna got up and let Angie catch it in her mouth. I watched as they licked each other to their third orgasms on the bed beside me. Then they took turns sucking my dick. Right after I came for the third time, I was out like a light.

I woke up to a sharp pain in my forehead. These crazy bitches were cutting me and laughing like psychopaths! I passed out from the pain. When I woke up again, they were gone and the ropes had been untied. I grabbed my clothes and got the fuck out of there.

When I got home and saw my forehead, I was pissed. The word "LIAR" was gonna be my scar for a long time. I been wearing hats ever since.

Six months later, I saw those crazy bitches walking through the grocery store together. When they saw me, Creshawna reached over and rubbed Angie's swollen belly. I tugged my hat down a little and looked the other way. They laughed.

This is the first time I've told this story to anybody...probably the last too. *Who's gonna believe me anyway?* Do you?

Keno Said It...

Having multiple partners or inviting a third person into your relationship seems to be trending now. Yes, the experience has its rewards; but it also has so many possible ways it could go wrong. Is the relationship really strong enough to withstand those possible outcomes? Are you and your partner both trustworthy enough stay within the agreed upon boundaries? Is this arrangement being made to supposedly "save" the relationship? Another person comes along with another personality to adjust to, another set of emotions to consider, motives you need to be clear and aware about, and new sexual chemistry. Are you really ready for this? Or, are you just interested in more sex? Don't jump into this type of situation then get mad at the resulting consequences of that decision.

"If you only knew, no other man could take me from you."

-A woman who's fucking her best friend when you leave.

The Sacrifices We Make

I think most men would love to be in a relationship where he can have two woman and no drama. I mean, for most of us... that's living like a king. My wife and I had discussed the possibility of adding a third before we got married, we just hadn't actively pursued the idea. So, when she came to me a year ago saying she found someone we should give a chance, you can imagine my excitement.

Not only was I going to be able to enjoy another woman, but my wife would be able to enjoy me enjoying her. Now, I know what you're thinking. This type of relationship comes with a lot more than the pleasure. I knew that going into it. I knew I'd have to do whatever it would take to keep not just my wife happy, satisfied and emotionally intact; but I'd have to do all those same things for our third while maintaining whatever our agreed upon balance is between the two. In my mind, I could handle it.

I was more than ready, but the wife took a little convincing. We started off with a conversation. "It's not really my thing." She said. "I would only be doing it for you. I'm not even sure I want to eat pussy."

"Well, how do you know you don't like it if we don't try it." I asked. After talking about it for so long, I was going to have this whether she wanted it or not; I just didn't want to have to actually cheat on her to get it. I told myself, *if she's smart, she'll let me do it my way and save herself some heartache.*

She shot me a look like she could read my mind. She squinted her eyes as if to say, *nigga I know what you're up to.* But shit... she did know what I was up to. Either we were going to fuck a bitch together or I was going to fuck two without her. I shot her a look back. I knew damn well she didn't want to go back to me cheating on her sensitive crying ass.

"I'll do it for you, baby." She softened. "But... it has to be her because I met her first."

"I mean, I just want you to be comfortable with everything." I told her.

"I know; and with her, I will be." She smiled all of a sudden and for a second, I wondered if this had anything to do with me at all.

I brushed the thought aside. "I think so too, bae. So, let me see her." I said reserving my excitement until I knew she was my physical type.

My wife handed me her phone and on the screen was a picture of a thick woman with a golden-brown complexion, full hips and lips and a slim waist. I swiped to the next picture and she was in a lavender lace panty and bra set. Her ass-to-titty ratio was damn near perfect and the look in her eyes said she was nasty. My dick was already getting hard.

My baby came up behind me and slid her hands down to grab my dick. "I see you like her already."

"Yeah, baby. She looks good." I confessed.

"I know... my pussy got so wet the first time we met."

I turned to face her. "Oh yeah, can't wait to lick on that pussy, huh?" I kissed her lips then her neck.

"Mmmm. I can't wait to have those soft looking lips of hers wrapped around my clit." She said as she wrapped her arms around my neck. We made love for two hours that night; we were that excited about this woman.

A week or two later, wifey started a group chat for the three of us. The shit was lit. Nudes from both of their fine asses, texting all day and one night out of nowhere we had phone sex.

I just knew this shit was going to work. So, I did it. I invited her over to spend a night with us. Wifey was all for it. She cosigned immediately and the plans were set.

She came over and the night was everything I wanted it to be. They took turns sucking my dick. I ate more pussy than I ever had in one night; and to my surprise my wife loved watching me fuck her. I came so hard and so many times that I collapsed when we finally stopped. It was the best night of my life. The wife said she felt the same. The next morning, we all had breakfast like we were used to waking up to each other. So, we did it again the next weekend... and the next. It became a regular thing.

Six months in, things were going better than any of us could have expected. We were having date nights, the girls got to spend time without me once a week and sex between the wife and I had never been better.

Then, it happened. My wife got sent away on business for a week. It was only one week. She and I just didn't make plans with her and we thought we would just pick up where we all left off the following week. The first six days went by without a hitch. We still texted in the group chat; but I swear I didn't plan what happened next.

On the last day of my wife's trip, I was lying in bed watching TV when the doorbell rang. I glanced at the clock. "Who the fuck is this?" I asked myself, knowing I wasn't expecting anybody. By the time I got to the door, they were ringing the bell again. "Who is it?" I yelled.

"It's Thursday. Who else would it be?" Her voice made my dick jump.

I opened the door. "Stacy. What are you doing here?"

She kissed my lips and walked past me, letting herself in. "I thought you two thought more of me than to just skip our time together."

"You know Unique is away on business." I was confused.

She took her short trench coat off and she was completely naked. "So, because she's gone, I don't get time with either of you?" She walked over to me. "Didn't you miss me?"

My eyes danced all over her body. Her titties were sitting right with her nipple poking. Her thighs and ass looked soft as hell; just like I knew they were. I didn't say a word; my mind was too busy collecting reasons my wife wouldn't be mad. She knew I was fucking her because we fucked her together. It was Thursday, if she were home... we would have been fucking her anyway.

"Hello?" She interrupted my thinking. "I said, didn't you miss me." She took my hand and put it on her ass. "Didn't you miss all of this?"

"Mmhmm." I mumbled.

"What?" She leaned in and kissed my neck.

"Yes." The word escaped my lips and I took a step back. "You gotta leave, Stacy."

"Why?" She walked over to the couch, spread her legs and started rubbing her clit.

"You know my wife is out of town. We will see you next week." The words came out correctly but my eyes were glued to her fingers as they glided back and forth on her clit.

"Umhm." She smiled. "Come suck on it. I'll leave after I cum. I promise."

I knew I shouldn't. My gut was in knots but my feet carried me over to that couch. I caressed her foot and continued to watch in silence. I could hear how wet she was from where I was standing. Shit sounded like hot macaroni and cheese.

"Come on." She begged. "I'm so horny."

I kept watching but my hand had slipped down to rub her calf.

"I can feel your tongue on my pussy already. Please." She moaned.

I sat next to her on the couch and rubbed her thigh. That pussy sounded so juicy it had my mouth watering. "You have to leave as soon as we finish." I bargained more with myself than with her.

"Okay." She agreed spreading her legs wider.

I got on my knees and let her press that dripping wet pussy against my tongue and grind on my face. My dick was so hard, it felt like it would burst open. I kept licking as her moans got louder and louder.

"Oh my gosh... yes... Don't stop. Lick it just like that. I'm gonna cum all over your face." She moaned.

"Umhmm." I started sucking her clit.

We got so into it that neither of us heard the door open and shut. I was licking and sucking; I had even licked her ass a few times. Showing the fuck off! She couldn't handle it, she started tapping my head. I looked up at her and her eyes were wide. She was about to cum hard. I was licking and sucking and out of nowhere I felt a tap on my shoulder.

It scared the shit out, if I'm keeping it a hundred; just because I knew we were in the house alone when I started. Turning around and finding my wife standing over us was a whole different feeling. I know my heart skipped a few beats. I wasn't sure how she was going to react; but to my surprise, she got down on her knees beside me and picked up where I had left off. I couldn't have planned it better myself.

After watching for a few minutes, I got up and walked over to the other end of the couch. I leaned in and kissed her lips, slipping my tongue between them. She moaned into my mouth and I heard my wife moan right after. If my dick got any harder, I'd be able to cut diamonds with it. So, I stood up and shoved my dick into her mouth.

We switched three times before we got up and made our way to the bedroom. That's where the ladies took over. We didn't even bother turning on the lights; we were so wrapped up in kissing, licking, and sucking on whoever our mouths could reach. I ended up on my back on the bed while their tongues wrestled around my dick.

Without saying a word, one of them tied my ankles to opposite corners at the foot of our California king-sized bed. I was all for whatever they had come up with, so I didn't protest when my hands got tied to opposite corners of the headboard. I was thinking, *let the games begin*. Then the lights came on.

"What's wrong?" I asked them.

Stacy shook her head. "Like I told you, this nigga ain't shit. We should have kept our arrangement at my place. Look at this disloyal nigga."

"What the fuck is going on? What arrangement? What the fuck are you talking about?" I looked from Stacy to my wife who was pulling her clothes from our dresser and throwing them into a suit case she had pulled from the closet. "Baby, what are you doing?"

She didn't respond; she didn't even look at me. She just kept packing.

"Should I tell him or do you want to?" Stacy said with a chuckle.

I felt lost and in the dark...and was growing angrier by the second. "Bitch, tell me what?"

She walked out of the room and came back with a man I had never seen a day in my life.

I struggled to sit up some. "What the fuc-"

"Let me introduce you to my husband, Juan. Also known as the guy that fucks us every day accept Thursdays." She looked at him like he was her childhood hero. "He's the definition of loyalty."

"Why the fuck is he here... in my house? And why are you packing?" I was pissed.

Stacy kept talking like she didn't hear shit I said. "Last night, we tried his chin. Your sweetie here..." She walked over and slapped my wife on the ass. "Knocked on my door late last night. Neither of us opened it. I just told her through the door that she had to stick to the rules. It was something she already knew. We have been doing this for too long."

My wife stopped for a second and looked at her with apologetic eyes. They kissed and she went back to packing.

Stacy continued. " Anyway... long story short. Disloyalty will be rewarded with disloyalty. So, we have another surprise for you." She looked over at my wife who nodded in agreement.

"Look, I don't know what the fuck y'all on-" I started but was cut off when I saw the worse shit I could have seen.

My wife walked over to Stacy's husband, got on her knees in front of him and pulled his dick from his pants. I tugged at the rope trying to get free, but it was no use. All I could do was watch as my wife shoved his dick down her throat. I could tell she had done it before because Juan was two times bigger than me and she was taking it in like a pro.

My heart ached like somebody I loved had died right there in front of me. I watched as this man lifted my wife up with her legs dangling over his forearms and fucked my lady like a porn star. A smile grew on Stacy's lips as she watched along with me. She even pinched one of her own nipples as her husband let my wife down gently and bent her over.

Hearing her moan in pain and pleasure was like daggers to my eardrums. I could tell she was cumming over and over again. I kicked and pulled, trying my hardest to break free of that fucking rope. I wanted to killed that muthafucka. Him and his bitch. I just couldn't break loose.

Stacy leaned in and kissed my forehead. I jerked my whole body trying to get to that bitch. She laughed and turned to walk away. I shed a few tears watching the three of them take my wife's belongings and walk out. I was still trying to figure out how the fuck I had gotten to this point when I heard the door slam shut behind them.

I have never treated a bitch the same. Never trusted one again and will never get married again. When you see me out here dawgin these bitches, mind your business… I been through some shit.

Keno Said It...

I hear women venting all the time about what their ex did to them. How he lied, cheated, or used her. I'm not condoning damaging anybody. I'm just saying that a person can only continue to do to you what you let them do. If he "kept lying", you kept letting him lie to you. If he "was cheating", you let him continue to cheat on you by allowing him to still have access to you after you found out. After you find out they did you wrong the first time... EVERY other time they do it to you is your fault. Don't shoot the messenger ladies!

"What goes around, comes around."

-A woman who will make sure it comes
back around for that ass.

A Bitch Named Carmen (Karma)

"This house is nice... and it's big. You stay here by yourself?" Kayla asked and I knew she already knew the answer.

"No, I have a roommate." I told her. Shit my girl was something like a roommate, right? I mean, we shared the house, right? Anyway, the truth about my situation was none of her business really. All she needed to know was how I liked my dicked sucked and not to call if I ain't hit her line first. "This sundress got your ass looking good." I slapped her ass and changed the subject all at once.

"Thank you." She had the nerve to blush. "I bought it to wear just for you."

How nice. I thought dryly, but instead, I said, "Take that shit off." I started to strip down myself. I knew we ain't have too much time before my girl came back. Maybe two to three hours tops.

"Damn, can't wait to get it, huh?" She smiled as she began to undress.

"Exactly." I said, laying on the bed completely naked.

She climbed into bed beside me and started kissing my neck.

"Save those kisses for him." I told her as a cuffed her chin with my finger.

"Okay." She submissively whispered. Then she scooted down and put herself between my legs.

95

"Sit that ass up so I can see it." I commanded.

She did as she was told and slowly slid my dick into her mouth and as far back as she could handle.

I closed my eyes and let my head fall back. Her head was amazing. It felt good, but the sloppy slurping sounds she made did it for me. After just fifteen minutes, I shot my load down her throat and dared her to spit it out. She swallowed and open her mouth to show me how much of a "good girl" she was.

"You ready to cum on it?" I asked her.

"Yes."

"Get that muthafucka back hard." I have to admit. The real appeal with her was that she listened. My girl was a boss. Not just in her career but shit...I couldn't command shit from her even in the bedroom. A nigga had to ask. This chick bent and folded to my will and it made me feel like a man. NO. It made me feel like THE man.

She sucked my dick until it was hard and pulsating in her mouth. Then I bent that that ass over and gave her her reward.

Another twenty minutes later, I was walking her back out to her car. "Thank you for pulling up on me. It was just what I needed."

She smiled. "Don't take forever to invite me back." She said as she got into her car.

"I got you." I told her.

She pulled off and I called my girl to see how much time I had.

"Hey." She said dryly.

"You on your way back?" I asked.

"Why?" She replied, rightfully suspicious.

I wasn't going to give it way though. "I should've come with you."

"Yeah, I guess you should have. What you doing?" She asked.

"Standing outside smoking." I told her.

"Oh aight. I'll be back in a few." She said.

I heard a car approaching so I looked up and it was her. I couldn't help thinking, *she thinks she's slicker than me.*

Carmen pulled up with her eyes locked in on me. I knew she didn't trust me and if I'm being honest, she shouldn't because Ima always do my thing; but I wasn't about to let that shit slide.

"Why you ain't you say you were pulling up?" I asked her as she got out.

"Because I was pulling up. I don't have to announce that I'm coming to my own house. Why? Is that what you called me for. To see how close I was?"

"No." I lied. "I know you don't trust me...but try to make it less obvious. Please?" I laid it on thick.

Carmen stopped short of the door. She didn't say anything or look my way, she just stopped walking and stood there.

"I'm just saying." I added and pulled hard on my cigarette.

She dropped her head and I knew what that meant. She turned around slowly. "You're right." She mumbled. "I'm sorry." She walked towards me.

"Nah. You're not, but I understand." I said, knowing she was already feeling guilty.

"No. I am. I apologize. I have to try harder to trust you more." She said. Then kissed the corner of my mouth and turned to go inside.

"Don't try, baby. Do." I made sure to say before she disappeared onto the house and closed the door behind her.

I stayed out for a few minutes longer finishing my cigarette. I thought about whether or not I should feel guilty but before the verdict came in... she was calling my phone. "Yeah." I answered.

"I'm getting in the shower then I'm going to start dinner. Steak and shrimp?" It was her way of really apologizing.

"Sounds good. I'll be in in a minute." I told her and hung up.

I walked in five minutes later and she was in the shower. Something told me to look around the bedroom one more time to make sure the coast was really clear. Good thing I did. The bitch had left her wallet. *How the fuck do you leave your wallet?* I knew right away that the shit was intentional.

I put the wallet in a bag in a closet on the other side of the house. Then I got comfortable on the bed.

Half an hour later, she came out the bathroom with a cloud of steam following her. Carmen was naked and I was just barely attracted to her. It wasn't that she wasn't cute. She was just bigger than I usually like my women; but I couldn't pass on being with her because she was one of the realest chicks I knew at the time. Plus, she had that check. I had taken care of every female I had been with until her. So, yeah.... I was letting her big ass take care of me.

She must've seen my thoughts written on my face because she rushed to put something on. "I'm going to start dinner." A hint of sadness in her voice.

"Okay. I can't wait to eat." I told her. The bitch could cook too. Everything she had made me tasted amazing.

Carmen flashed a quick smile and left the room. Not even a minute later, I heard her 90s RnB blasting.

I texted my other bitches while she cooked. I kept at least five of them. In hindsight, I should've stayed down with her; but in the moment I could only think of what I didn't like about her and no matter how much shit I did like ...it just wasn't enough.

Before long, she had the house smelling all kinds of good. I walked into the kitchen and found her singing as she made our plates.

Dinner was actually pleasant. I could tell she was making a real effort to be nice, but really, that was part of the problem. I'm used to my bitches falling over themselves in love with me. She loved me and I knew that; but not the way I wanted her to. Not the way a man like me deserves.

Anyway, I showered after dinner and we laid in bed together. Those moments were peaceful. So much so that it itched my panic button. I needed fire, excitement.

We attempted to have sex. When I say "attempted", I mean we fucked but honestly, Carmen was way too advanced for me. I never could last more than ten minutes with her. The pussy was good; but she did too much. She liked that kinky shit. A nigga tried but...I don't know...I just wasn't there and Carmen didn't help. I felt less than when I was fucking her. My other bitches let me dick them down. No demands, no bossing me around, and no expectations of things I have never experienced before. Just dick.

I came so hard and so fast that I didn't have to question whether or not she was satisfied. I already knew that she wasn't; and that's why I knew that she cheating too.

She tried to pacify me. "I liked it."

I knew she was lying. "You don't gotta lie."

She got quiet. Then she said, "Let's not make it a bigger deal than it really is. Please? Let's just lay and watch a movie."

I agreed. I actually enjoyed laying with her. I just didn't do it too often because I would be sleeping all the time, fucking with her. I got into bed and she wrapped herself around me. Next thing I knew, I was waking up the next morning.

It was 4 am. I got up and got dressed. She was sound asleep and worked for herself so she didn't have to wake up for a while. So, I crept out.

I initially went out just to gamble a little. Then I got a call from Alicia. She was my older chick. She was about 40 but her and her kids still lived at her mom's place. It sounds fucked up; but the fact that she ain't have shit of her own made her easy to please. We just had to link late nights or early in the morning. "Yeah." I answered.

"I'm about to pull up. Come outside." She purred.

"I ain't there. Go home. I'll pull up on you. Meet you there." I hung up without waiting for her to agree because she did whatever I told her to do.

I pulled up in front of her mother's house and she gave me the sloppiest head I've ever gotten right there in the car. Then she road my dick until we both came. With her, I lasted 25 minutes.

We matched blunts and sat and talked. Before I knew it, the sun was coming up and my phone was ringing off the hook.

I already knew she was in the house fuming. She usually was; but I couldn't be tamed. She had to come to that understanding.

I got home around eight in the morning and was met with full on rage. She threw a glass candleholder at my face and barely missed. She threw a frying pan, even the iron. Then she came at me with her hands.

"YOU WANT TO ACT LIKE YOU SINGLE?! COMING AND GOING LIKE YOU DONT GIVE A FUCK?! FINE! GET YO SHIT AND GET THE FUCK OUT MY HOUSE?!" She yelled as we tussled. When we stepped away from each other, she was crying. "Just get the fuck away from me. Just go. Why are you here if this is what you're gonna do?"

Like usual, after we fought… we made love. I followed her into the bedroom and pushed her onto the bed. I ripped her clothes off of her and buried my face in her pussy.

She fought me at first; but by the second time she came she was soft and submissive and back to crying.

"I'm sorry." I mumbled as I came up to push myself inside her.

"No. Stop. I just want you to go." She cried. "I need you to go."

"No." I told her as I wrapped her legs around my waisted and slow stroked her. "I'm not leaving."

She cried until her sobs became moans. That took about fifteen minutes. After we fought was the only time I could last inside her. It was the only time she wasn't aggressive. I knew that was only because she felt guilty about all the aggressive shit she would do when we fought; but if she would have been like that more often, we would still be together now.

Anyway. We fell asleep again. She cooked, we ate and fell back to sleep. We woke up and ate again and went back to sleep. We pretty much slept the rest of the day away. Then about 11 pm came and I knew I had to do something to make up with her.

So, I went into the living room and pushed the couches together. I lit candles all around the room and pulled a blanket from the closet.

Just like I knew she would, she came into the living room to see what I was doing. When she saw it, she fought the smile trying to emerge on her face.

"You like it?" I asked, even though I already knew the answer.

She didn't respond. She just walked over to where I was.

I laid her down, warmed some oil and massaged her whole body. Then I made her cum over and over again...on my fingers, my tongue and then finally my dick. Just when I thought I had her right where I wanted her... my phone rang.

She looked at her phone to check the time. "Who is that?"

I didn't know; but I did know it was for sure a bitch.

She got up and headed to get my phone. I didn't even attempt to follow her. It just was what it was. I was tired of lying any way.

She came back stomping every step of the way. "Who the fuck is Angela?"

"A chick I'm fucking on the side. It's nothing serious though." I sat down.

She plopped down across from me. She must have been just as tired of fighting as I was. "A bitch. She's A bitch you're fucking on the side?!"

"Yeah." I looked into her eyes.

She dropped her head. "Okay. How many bitches are you fucking on the side?"

"Five." I held my gaze.

She just stared for a long moment. Then she spoke softly. "Five? You're fucking five other bitches?"

"Yeah." I was genuinely surprised she hadn't flipped and thrown something yet.

"Okay." She said as she began to go through my phone. Neither of us said a word. I watched her as she found everything she was looking for and her face changed with each discovery. "I want you to leave." She said, calmer than I had ever seen her. "Get all your shit and go. Please. We can't keep doing this shit. I can't keep doing this with you. Just go." Tears were welling in the corners of her eyes. She used her fingers to stop them from falling.

"No." I told her.

"What the fuck do you mean, no?!" She yelled. Then immediately calmed herself. "Look, you're obviously not into me like I thought; and to be honest...you're not exactly what I want for myself either." She moved her hands to look into my eyes.

"I'm not leaving. You're mine." I said.

"Right, and you mishandle everything that's yours. I'll pass. I want out. I'm done." She told me and I could see how serious she was.

"Fuck you then." I got up and went collecting my shit. Don't get me wrong. I knew I was mishandling her, but she was mine to mishandle. Shit, they all were.

Usually she would be yelling and screaming, throwing things and all in emotional disarray. I knew what to do with that version her; but I didn't know to do with this calm, collected and decisive version of her.

I threw all my shit in a big bin from a closet and walked out the door. When I looked up and saw her standing at the door, I was sure she had come to her senses.

"My key." She said dryly.

"What?" I hissed.

"Give me my key back." She stood on her decision.

I snatched my keys out my pocket, pulled her house key off and threw it at her; then I hopped into my car and sped off.

An hour later, I still hadn't heard from her. So, I texted her. **Can I sleep in the den? I'll find somewhere to stay in the morning. It's the middle of the night.** She didn't respond but I knew she had read it. So, I texted again. **If you ever loved me like you said you did, I think I deserve at least that.**

My phone said she was typing... Then she stopped. I started to send another message ... **Well fuck you then fat, ugly, bit-**...but she answered back before I could send it.

The side door is unlocked

I knew I had her. If she was willing to let me back in, I would be in the bed with her by morning. I hate to say it, but this was exactly why I was dragging her like I was. In certain areas, she was a boss...but at the same time, in other areas she was weak.

I woke up the next morning holding her. I was in the middle of thinking of how to "make up" to her this time when the doorbell rang. I just knew it wasn't for me; so, I laid there and let her get it.

A few minutes passed, and I heard a scream. I jumped up and ran to the living room. What I saw shocked me. She had a Ruger in her hand aimed at a light skin petite woman curled up on the floor.

"Baby, what the fuck?" I walked over to her and tried to take the gun from her hand. To my surprise she turned the barrel in my direction.

"Get down on the floor with your bitch."

"What?" She had me fucked up.

She shot into the wall inches away from the woman who started crying loudly.

I got down and finally got a look at the woman's face. "Reina, what the fuck are you doing here?"

"Dying, muthafucka. Right with yo stupid ass." She whispered and I heard the gun go off.

I woke up three days later in a hospital room disoriented and in so much pain that I was afraid to move. I still can't believe the bitch shot me. I only did what she let me do.

"Most niggas ain't shit."

-A woman who keeps dating the same kind of man and generalizing "most niggas".

Keno's Story

Reintroduction...

A lot has been said so far. I've given away a lot of the game. Too much of it; I know I'm getting kick out the game for this; but all the advice... the moral of all the stories told here is this. There are so many reasons why we men do the things we do. It's easy to say we ain't shit and leave it at that when you almost never know how we got to that point. Most of the time, the women dawgin' us for not being what they wanted or expected have no clue about the why.

The why would explain all our foul decisions away. I know the stories you've heard so far have you saying "Damn, these niggas really ain't shit"; and truth be told...some of us ain't. All I'm saying is that there are a few of us with good reason behind it all.

I'm not speaking for every man because I don't know them or what the fuck they be doing. I'm speaking for myself right now. In my case... and I know in some if the homies' cases... y'all are the cause.

I ain't shit! I'll be the first to admit that but relationships are two-way streets. Here is my why.

Chapter 1

The smell of her perfume danced in front of my nose as I kissed her neck. Her whispered sigh tickled my ear drum; and her soft lips pressed on my shoulder made my dick jump. She hadn't been mine in years but every time she let me have her for the night, it was like this. She just did something to me.

Her five-foot-two frame was stacked with curves and I could never keep my hands off of her when we were anywhere near each other. Five minutes alone and... you know the rest. I can't even say she was my weakness because a muthafucka would get super-strength standing up in that pussy and walk away feeling like I was on top of the world.

Every man has that one woman that does this to them. The one woman that even happily married, they couldn't resist. The one woman who we would fuck up even the best situation to get a little time with. No man alive (or dead) would blame me for how this shit went down.

Carla had been my high school sweetheart. Her body had been my secret addiction for as long as I was fucking. She walked out of my house three years ago saying how I wasn't taking her seriously because she caught me cheating again. I didn't think she was serious, but she never came back to stay.

So, having her in my arms again brought back so many feelings that I could never tell her. Feelings that I still wasn't ready to face. Not yet. I love Carla... always have, always will. I just wasn't ready to be the family man she wanted me to be and she had to accept that. If the feeling was mutual, she would wait.

I kissed her shoulders and chest as I brushed the straps of her dress aside. Her breasts sat perky and poking out the top of her strapless-bra. I kissed and licked her cleavage.

She put her hands on my chest. "Keno."

I ignored her fake protest. As I gently lifted her right breast so her nipple appeared, my mouth immediately started to water. I traced her areola with my tongue before sucking her hardening nipple into my mouth and heard her gasp in a gust of air.

"Keno. Stop." She pushed me away. "It's always about sex with you. Did you even think about what I said?"

"Yeah, I thought about it." I confessed as I pulled her back to me.

"And?" She stepped away, staring me in my eyes like all hope was lost.

"I ain't gonna be something I'm not. Not for you... Not for anybody." I pulled her close again. "Stop playing like this ain't what you want. Why else would you be here?"

She shook her head and pressed her forehead to my chest as if she really had to think about the answer. Then, just like I knew she would, she gave in. She let me take her clothes off and the sight of her body made my dick hard enough to break bricks. Her body was everything I remembered it being; soft, sweet-smelling and wet as ever. Her mouth was amazing; her head kept my toes curling. Her pussy was and still is the best I've ever had. I said she gave in but I struggled not to. From the moment I slid inside her, I wanted to cum. I had to fight just to last in the pussy.

When I felt her body buckle under me, I was relieved. I wouldn't let myself cum before her. If she needed a reason the keep thinking about me when she left, it was my duty to give her one. With her legs trembling around my waist, I pulled out. She looked confused until I pushed her legs back and leaned in to slide my tongue over her wetness. She struggled to breath until I came back up and shoved my hardness back inside her. She was even wetter after cumming on my tongue. Knowing she had cum twice, I felt like finally… I could too. I came so hard that it felt like my soul left my body with it.

Usually, we laid together and talked for a while. This time, she got up and stayed in the bathroom so long that I knew something was wrong.

"You okay in there?" I called to her from the bed. She didn't respond. "Carla?!" I called again before getting up and walking to the bathroom door. "Carla?"

"I came to tell you about your son." She said from the other side of the door.

I laughed. "Baby, I know I'm good; but it doesn't work that fast."

"He's almost two years old, muthafucka." I heard her voice crack. "I was hoping so badly that you had changed. That you deserved the family I been wanting so bad but you haven't. You still that same nigga." I heard her crying.

"Open the door, Carla." It was all I could manage to say. I knew we had made a baby but she kept telling me, 'if we did I ain't keeping it'. When she didn't say anything, I assumed we had lucked out.

"I'm sorry I came." She said as I heard her moving around but not opening the door.

"Open the door." I demanded, anger building inside me. "Why the fuck would you keep this shit from me? I missed my son being born? His first steps and word? All that good shit just because yo ass got a point to prove? Open the fuckin door!"

She snatched open the door fully dressed. I hadn't even seen her pick her clothes up off my floor where I left them. She stormed past me. "Yeah, you missed all of that and you gonna keep missing shit. You told me you weren't ready for a family, so who the fuck was I to give you one?" She grabbed her purse and headed for my door.

I moved quicker than I had in a long time. I grabbed her by her hair and pulled her toward me. "Where the fuck are you going?"

She looked me dead in my eyes and said, "Do it. Hit me. You only gonna show me I was righter than I thought."

I let her hair go. "Carla, I-"

She cut me off. "I waited a long time for you to be ready. Did you think I would wait forever? When I found out I was pregnant, I was so happy until I realized you probably wouldn't even want me to keep it. Just forget I told you. I won't come back." She walked out the door and I just let her ass go.

It was nights like this one that I wondered why I did. Nights when no pussy was deep enough to make me fall out of remembering her eyes when she said it. Nights when even the best throat couldn't distract me from my thoughts. Nights like this, I wondered what stopped me from stopping her. The bitch was dead ass wrong for keeping my son from me; but was she right about me?

Even with my helmet on, the wind was hitting. The blur of everything passing by as I zipped through the city was one of the reasons I loved riding. Going one hundred and ten miles an hour on the highway was the only time my head felt clear. Sometimes, you need to go fast to slow down, I guess.

Watching the scenery fly by, I got lost in my thoughts. The sound of her voice was still ringing in my ears. "Did you think I would wait forever?" Hell yeah, I thought she would wait as long as it took. She was supposed to ride for a nigga. I kept telling myself, "Fuck her", but really every night I thought about fucking her.

The road usually took my mind off of it. I could refocus my shit and by the time I got back, I would be good. Not tonight though. It had been 45 minutes and I was still thinking about her. So much that I almost didn't see the lights coming towards me.

Now, I know I zoned the fuck out but I was in my lane. The stupid muthafucka driving a 16-wheeler commercial truck had to be asleep at the wheel because he was in the wrong lane coming right toward me. Everything happened so fast that I couldn't react. I saw the lights, then I saw the wheels. Then everything went black.

Chapter 2

I woke up days later in the hospital. I had three broken ribs, a punctured lung, a broken leg, a fracture wrist, a dislocated shoulder, and a concussion... plus too many cuts, scrapes, and road burn. My entire body was stiff as hell; still, I was just glad to be alive. I thought for sure that truck was going to be the end of me.

When I opened my eyes, I didn't want to move or speak. I knew at any minute the pain was going to kick up and I knew that was gonna be a muthafucka. I just looked around, taking in my surroundings.

The lights were bright as hell. So bright that I didn't notice it was night until my eyes landed on the blinds in the window and I could see the glow of the street lights. The walls were white. Crispy white; clean. They gave me a little relief because they gave me hope that I had landed in a good hospital. The sheet and blanket over me felt soft and looked clean too. I was almost comfortable. The sound of my monitors beeping at a consistent pace was reassuring and if it wasn't for the tube down my throat preventing me from taking a deep breath, I would have sighed my relief.

Just as I started to choke... which really made me feel alive... an angel walked in. She reminded me of Gina from Martin. Her light skin almost glowed against the crisp white of her nursing scrubs. Her hair was cut short and not a hair was out of place. Her clothes fit her body perfectly. Every curve accentuated. They were tight enough that they looked painted on but not so tight that it looked like she was doing too much. I got a good look at her as she walked to my monitors with her clipboard and wrote something down.

She glanced over at me and was caught by surprise. "Oh! You're awake." She came over to me and took the tube from my throat gently. I coughed and she rushed out of the room. I wondered where she went but I didn't have to wonder for long. She came back into the room with a small plastic cup and held it to my lips. I stared into her hazel brown eyes as I sipped. "Your throat will be a little sour for the first few hours but the pain will go away on its own." I just stared at her as she leaned in over me and the smell of her perfume found my nose.

She moved away and we locked eyes. I must have been attempting to smile because she smiled back. "I see the meds are still working for you." I nodded my head in response. "Good." She put something into my hand and I held onto her fingers for a second. She chuckled. "That's the call button. Call me if you need me. The doctor has you scheduled to be on a liquid diet for a few days but breakfast isn't until 6:30." I looked around for a clock. "It's just after midnight." She told me.

I nodded and she patted my hand before saying, "I was praying for you to pull through." Then she left my room, leaving the door cracked.

I sat there thinking about the accident. I had no clue what actually happened; but how was I supposed to find out? I slowly peeled the covers back to get a look at myself. The bandages around my chest had me thinking I could already feel the pain that was coming. I had a cast on my right arm and my left leg and an ace bandage wrapped around my left wrist. Moving the covers with my left arm was smooth; but when I tried to move my right arm, a sharp pain made me wince which helped me find out every other part that hurt. So, I pulled the covers back over me and laid there as still as I could.

I wondered how long I had been out and if I still had a bike. I wondered what happened to the stupid muthafucka driving the truck. Then after a while, as they usually did when I sat still for too long, my thoughts went to Carla and… my son.

I wondered what he looked like. I wondered what his personality was like; what it might be like to spend time with them both. I started to piss myself off wondering why that wasn't something Carla wanted. So, I was too glad when I felt myself falling back to sleep; but the fucked-up thing about your thoughts is that you can never escape them.

I dreamed about her. About fucking her. I had a whole wet dream about the bitch like I was back in high school. The shit was so realistic that when the nurse touched me to wake me up for breakfast, my shit was standing up and the blanket and sheet were visibly wet. I was so damn embarrassed. I know she noticed; she couldn't have missed the way my shit was reaching for the sky but she pretended not to see it.

"I brought you some soup. I'm not sure how good it is; but I know it'll feel good going down. And I know you're starving." She sat the tray on a table beside the bed and raised my bed so I could sit up some. The shit hurt like hell but I wasn't going to let her see me show it. She looked at me and made a face.

After a few seconds, she said, "Oh shit!" She reached over and pushed a button attached to my IV. "I'm so sorry. You must be in so much pain. I should have increased your meds as soon as I knew you were awake. Are you okay?"

I gave her a weak smile. She gently hit herself in the forehead and pulled up a chair beside my bed. "I'm so sorry. I don't know where my mind is. I'm going to feed you some of this soup. Just touch my hand when you're done eating, okay?" She sat down in the chair.

I was so focused on making my dick lay down that I couldn't even acknowledge that I had heard what she said.

116

"Did you hear me?"

I glanced at her face and nodded. Then I let my eyes drop back to the blanket.

"Okay." She said and opened a packet to retrieve a plastic spoon.

She fed me some of the nastiest soup I had ever tasted but she was right. It felt good going down. I hadn't even thought about how hungry I was. Without a single chunk of real food, it served the purpose of filling my stomach. Somewhat.

When I was satisfied that my dick had gone down, I looked up at her again. First, at her face. Her full bottom lip threatened all the work I had just done but I still let my eyes drop to her small breasts. Her name tag read "Shanetta". She followed my eyes to her name tag and said, "Shit, I didn't even introduce myself, did I? What the fuck am I doing tonight?" She shook her head and glanced away.

When our eyes met again, she said, "I'm Shanetta. I'm your nurse for this shift. I'll be here six days. Then I'm off on Sundays."

I watched her mouth as she spoke. A straight top row of pearly white teeth played peek-a-boo with me and her long natural eyelashes made her slanted eyes look seductive. I wondered what she was thinking when she got quiet but her tongue betrayed her when it popped out the corner of her mouth. She caught herself before she licked her lip; but it was too late, I had already peeped the scene.

She blushed and cleared her throat. "Are you always this attentive?"

I decided to try my voice. "Yeah." It cracked as I said it. I tried to clear it but it was a little painful.

She gave me another sip from the cup of water. "You don't have to say anything. I know it hurts."

I nodded.

"I hope you don't mind me talking to you. Just tap me if I start talking to much." She went back to pick up the spoon sitting in the soup bowl.

I gave her a weak smile.

She smiled back and I noticed a dimple in her right cheek. It was kind of sexy. "Cool. Can I call you Kevin?"

"Keno." I said in a raspy, low tone.

She touched my hand and shook her head. "I'm sorry, Keno. I'll try not ask any more questions."

She sat there with me for another 40 minutes talking about whatever came to her mind as she fed me. I sat there the entire time watching her mouth and her facial expressions and all I was thinking was how beautiful this woman was. Then, we were both silent as she sponge-bathed my entire body. I was embarrassed for a second time. I hadn't shitted but having her wipe my nuts while my dick was wrinkled and soft was way too intimate for my liking. I almost wanted it to get hard to save my pride but I didn't want her to feel like I was a pervert. She was gentle and I had never been handled like that before; so, I had to focused to stay soft. I found myself watching her at first, but when I saw her glance up at my face, I looked away.

When she was done, she covered me with the blanket and patted my leg. "Okay, Keno. You're all set. The doctor will be in to see you this morning. Just hit the call button if you need me."

118

I nodded and she left, leaving the door cracked. Alone with my thoughts again, I was surprised to find that they didn't go to Carla. Shanetta had left me with plenty to think about. She had talked about so many different things; she seemed to be almost as smart as she was beautiful.

My last thought before I fell back to sleep was that I needed to get her off my mind. I had more important things to think about than fucking my pretty nurse.

Chapter 3

I woke up a third time to a male voice. "Can you hear me, Mr. Lawson?"

I tried to clear my throat. "Yeah."

"Welcome back." He said dryly. "You were in one hell of an accident. Things were touch and go for a few days."

I tried to pull myself into a sitting position. After two failed attempts, I nodded for him to continue.

"You're pretty banged up and your vitals still need to stabilize a little more before I can be satisfied releasing you. Eventually, we will get you in for some physical therapy and if that goes well...you could go home in about three weeks." He looked at my monitors and scribbled something onto his clipboard. Then after a long pause, he turned toward me. "How are you feeling?"

I cleared my throat again. "As well as can be expected, I guess."

He nodded and I knew he understood.

Well, we are going to run a few tests, today and ongoing, to keep track of whether or not you're improving."

For the next 15 to 20 minutes, he explained things to me that I was not awake enough to follow. Then he scribbled on his pad again and left. I was just relieved to be able to go back to sleep. All of his touching and checking had brought back some of the pain that sweet nurse had drugged away.

I don't know how long I was out, but it was the smell of her perfume that woke me. The sweet fragrance danced into my nostrils and made my dick twitch in reaction.

"Oh, so you are awake." She said as she noticed the tent I was pitching under my blanket.

I cracked a slick grin; but my throat was too dry to even attempt speaking.

"Good afternoon." She said as she opened the curtains, letting in way too much sunlight.

I squinted and raised my arm to shield my eyes. Then I cleared my throat. "Could you leave those closed, please?"

"Nope. You need to wake up. How are you ever supposed to get better if you in here in the dark like you dying?" She walked back over to my bed.

I shrugged. She had a point, but the light was blinding.

She pulled back my blanket and sheets and checked my bandages and the sheets... totally disregarding my hard on. "Oh, you look okay." She covered me back up but stayed close. "I brought you some fresh water. Have some." She poured me a cup and I couldn't help but notice the design on her nails.

"Nice." I managed to say before taking a big gulp of water.

"What, these?" She looked at her own hands. "It's time to get them done again."

I glanced down wondering if she kept her toes done too. I'm not a feet loving man, there's just something about a pair of pedicured feet that turns me on. Anyway, when I looked up, we locked eyes.

"They're done too." She said.

The look in her eyes told me that she might actually take off a piece of clothing if I asked her to....at least her shoes and socks. I looked away. Like I said, I had more important things to do than to be trying to fuck my nurse.

"Do y'all have my phone tucked away somewhere?" I had to catch up with the outside world and find out who knew where I was and hadn't shown up or had been there while I was asleep.

"Ummm... yeah." She said, opening a closet cabinet on the other side of the room. "It should be in here with what's left of your clothes. We did have to cut some of the stuff off of you."

"Cut some of it off?" I repeated her.

"Yeah, you were unconscious when you came in. It wasn't like someone could have asked you to get undressed to save your clothes. The staff was more worried about saving your life." She handed me my phone.

I looked at my screen; it was completely dead. "How long was I out for?"

"Four days. You want to use my charger?" She offered.

"That would be great, if I'm not asking for too much." I told her.

"Not at all." She left my room and returned carrying her charger. She plugged it in and handed me the other end to plug into my phone.

"Thanks." I told her, flashing a weak smile.

"No problem. Just let me know when you're done with it or if you need something." She flashed a smile of her own and left.

I waited for my phone to power up. As I sat there, a sharp pain shot up into my right side. It caught me so off guard that I froze. I didn't want to move a muscle. It felt like I had been stabbed.

When the pain subsided, I picked up my phone and tried to figure out what I had missed. I checked my messages and emails and voicemail. Then I made a few calls. Once I was sure everyone knew about the situation that needed to know about it, I sat my phone down to charge up and laid down to rest a little more. I hit the button to increase my iv drip and let the pain killer take me back off to sleep.

Again, I don't know how long I was out because those meds understood the fucking assignment. They put me all the way down. When I woke up again, I woke up to the warm and wet sensation of a tongue twirling on the head of my dick. Her soft lips gripped my dick like they were made to wrap around me. I couldn't believe what was happening. Shorty had that vaccu-suck thing going on and the closer I got to cumming, the less like myself I felt.

I put my hand on the back of her head and gently guided her pace. From that angle, it looked like Carla had found me and come to her senses. So, I let my head drop back and enjoyed the feel of having what I wanted again.

She was really putting in work too. I mean, she was slurping and spitting, bobbing her head and letting me bounce off the back wall of her throat. I can honestly say I've never had an apology that good but... it's the only way I'll accept them from the women in my life moving forward. You're just not sorry enough if you're not sacrificing your esophagus to let me know it's real.

I ran my fingers through her hair and got the urge to stare into those big brown eyes of hers. I wanted to lock eyes with her while she sucked on me. I put the tips of my middle and ring finger under her chin and lifted it just enough to get her attention. When our eyes met, I was surprised to find my nurse looking up at me.

She didn't stop sucking. She stared into my eyes like she was soul-searching and sucked my dick like my cum would make her the richest woman alive.

I felt my body stiffen and I knew when I came, it was going to be explosive. With our eyes locked, she kept sucking until my entire body jerked forward. I opened my eyes to an empty room. *What the fuck was it about the hospital that had me wet dreaming like this?*

Chapter 4

I thought the next morning was going to be awkward. Especially, after dreaming she had sucked my dick; but surprisingly it wasn't. She came in unaware of my thoughts of her and went about the business of taking care of me. She bathed me, changed my bandages and gown and sat down to talk to me while I ate more of that nasty ass cafeteria soup.

"Do you remember any of the accident?" She asked.

"Pieces of it; but it's coming back the longer I'm awake." I confessed.

"So, what happened?"

"The truck driver must have fallen asleep at the wheel because he came into my lane. I didn't have enough time to react." I wasn't going to tell her I had taken my mind off the road.

"You need to speak to a lawyer. You should have a law suit on your hands. He was driving a company truck." She shook her head. "He was a couple rooms down for the first couple of days but his injuries were nothing compared to yours."

"The person at fault never gets hurt the worse." I said, realizing my throat wasn't sore anymore.

"True; but you need to get you a lawyer for sure." She told me. "They can come up here during visiting hours and get the ball rolling. Some of those suits take months."

"Yeah, I'll look into it tomorrow." I assured her.

"Good. You play cards?" She was clearly trying to lighten the moment.

"You don't want none of this. I'll whoop your ass in some Bid West." I chuckled and damn near choked on the pain that came after.

"Look at you, about to die on that lie." She laughed and it might have been the cutest shit I ever heard. She poured me a cup of water from a small plastic picture on a nearby table. "You alright?"

I took a few swallows of water. "Yes, I'm okay."

She got up and headed toward the door of my room. "Good, because you're in for a butt kicking when I come back with these cards."

She left cheerfully and I was starting to really like the energy she came with. She was pretty cool, but my mind kept bringing me back to how soft my dream had me believing her lips would feel. She got back just in time to stop my train of thought from carrying me away.

"You ready?" She asked, sitting down next to me with a smile.

Her long natural lashes lured me in again and when she looked up into my eyes, I was caught off guard. I looked away and cleared my throat.

She cleared hers too. "So, you ready for the butt whooping?"

"Only if you're ready to eat those words." I told her.

Shanetta shuffled the deck and dealt our hands between us. I picked up my cards and immediately flashed a smile thinking, *maybe we should bet something.*

126

Forty-five minutes later, I was holding my side and she is wiping tears from her eyes because we are laughing so hard.

"That is the dumbest thing I've ever heard." She said still laughing.

"I remember that." The familiar voice came out of nowhere.

We both looked up as if we had been caught in middle of fucking. I just knew my eyes were playing tricks on me when I saw Carla standing there.

"Carla?" I said as she walked over to my bed.

"Somebody told me you were in here and I had to come see that you were okay." She looked so sad as she took in the view of me laying in that hospital bed.

"Funny, you were the last person I expected to care." I couldn't help the sarcasm.

"How could you say that, Keno?" She gently laid her hand on my leg and looked into my eyes.

As I stared back into her eyes, Shanetta cleared her throat. "I'll let you two talk; it's time for me to clock out anyway."

I turned my attention back to Shanetta. "Thank you for everything you did today. See you tomorrow."

She flashed a weak smile. "See you tomorrow, Keno."

After Shanetta walked out -this time closing the door to my room, Carla sat down beside me.

"Friendly, isn't she?" She frowned.

"She's just doing her job." I said dryly. "I'll ask you again, what are you doing here? The last time I saw you, you were telling me I'd never see you again."

"Kevin, don't be like that. I came here to check on you. I was really worried you had…When I first heard about the accident, I thought…" She let her voice drift off.

"You thought I was dead; and you have a bunch of regrets." I said matter of factly.

"Yeah, I…" She started to say.

I cut her off. "Where's my son?"

"He's at my mother's house. I…" She started to explain.

I cut her off again. "Why didn't you bring him? Still don't think I deserve to see him?" I didn't intend to get angry. When I first saw her, I was genuinely glad to see her. Surprised, but glad. Now, the more she talked, the more upset I was becoming. This bitch really had me fucked up if she thought she could keep my son away from me. "Don't come back around me until you're ready to bring him with you."

"Kevin, are you serious? I …" Her eyes began to water.

"Bye." I said, staring her right in the eyes.

She turned to walk away, then turned back to face me. "If you send me away now…don't ever expect to see us."

"What, that wasn't your plan already?" I hissed.

She shook her head and walked out crying. Now, I know what you're thinking. Why would I treat her like that when she was on my mind so heavy after she left me? That's the problem. Bitches think they can make all the decisions when it comes to our kids and since she wanted to decide if I would be in his life…I got to decide if I would be in hers.

I sat there stewing in my anger for a while. It wasn't until the next nurse came in that I calmed down. All of what I estimated to be about 300 pounds of her waddled in. She handed me a piece of paper before walking to my monitors and scribbling on her board.

"I'm Colinda, your nurse for the rest of the day. I come in every other day. So, Ms. Monique will be taking over my shift on the days in between. Your vitals look good, Ms. Shanetta said you did well her whole shift. Let's keep that same energy, okay?"

"Alright." I agreed.

She walked over and checked my bandaged and sheets. "Can I get you something, Mr. Lawson?"

"Call me Keno." I told her. "And no, I'm okay."

"Okay, Mr. Lawson. Hit the call button if you need anything." She checked my IV. "What about your pain? Do you need me to increase your meds?"

"No, I feel fine. It's Keno." I said, trying to make myself believe she just didn't hear what I had said.

"Okay, Mr. Lawson. I'm right at the nurse's desk." She left out leaving my door wide open.

I called her back to close my door, but she kept walking like she didn't hear me. I opened the folded piece of paper she had hand me. It read:

Keno, I forgot to give you this number before I left. This is my sister's husband. He's and injury attorney. He's pretty good... not just because he's married to my sister either. Give him a call. 551-542-5422 Michael Shaub.

It was this gesture that changed my mood. It was such a nice thought. I called the number and was surprised to find out that the brother-in-law was actually a very reputable Jewish lawyer I had heard about once or twice. His retainer's fee was something I could manage and he agreed to come in to see me the next day.

I made a few other calls, including one to my mother. She quickly admitted to being the "somebody" who had told Carla where I was.

"What is wrong with you?" She scolded.

"Ma, you don't know the whole story." I said.

"I know my grandbaby deserves both of his parents." She said.

I was caught off guard thinking Carla hadn't told her. "You knew?"

"Not when he was born; but since your accident. Who do you think told her what hospital to find you at? I had the baby here while she came to talk to you; and when she came back and told me how you acted, I wanted to come up there and slap you myself."

"Why haven't you been up here, Ma?" I asked.

"I was up there the first three days; I was even up there right before you woke up. I was praying over you and talking to you. I was going to come today but when she came by with the baby, I wanted to give you two some time to talk. You mean to tell me God giving you this second chance at life and you're choosing to stay stubborn?" Her voice alone humbled me.

130

"Ma, I…"

She cut me off. "I don't want to hear it. That girl left town again. If she comes back, you better choose right. I'll be up there to see you after church on Sunday. I think you need some time to think." She said her peace and then told me she would call to check up on me the next day.

I ate more of that cafeteria soup and spent the rest of my waking hours deep in thought. *How was I the bad guy when this bitch was the one holding my son at a distance as if I'm somebody he needs to be protected from?*

Chapter 5

I fell asleep hoping for one of the wet dreams that I suffered before. Instead, my thoughts took me to a darker place. I opened my eyes to the old apartments I grew up in. I was watching myself eat a bowl of cereal as my mother and father argued in one of the back rooms. I remembered how I helpless I used to feel listening to the fight.

The closer I got to the kitchen table, the less like me the little boy at the table looked. I mean, he looked like me... but it wasn't me. I sat down beside him but he never looked up at me. I rubbed his head but he just kept eating his cereal.

I got up and walked towards the arguing. The closer I got to the back bedroom, the more one of the voices began to sound just like me. As I walked into the room, shock almost knocked me off my feet. I had Carla by her hair and she was desperately trying to get away from me.

It finally clicked in my mind. If it had been us arguing, then the little boy at the table wasn't me. I rushed back to the kitchen only to see the back of him as he walked out the door. I followed him but for some reason could not catch up. When I turned back around, Carla was laying on the floor out cold. *What the fuck?*

I jerked up out of my sleep in a cold sweat. That dream was so fucked up. My parent's relationship was sort of a soft spot and Carla and I have had a few spats, but I ain't no woman beater like my father and I damn sure ain't no killer. Plus, why the fuck would I have a dream where I'm the problem?

I sat up for a minute thinking about my situation with Carla. I guess there were some things I could have done differently. Still, I felt like keeping my son away from me for the first two years of his life made her a real bitch.

Nurse Colinda came in and checked on me and my vitals, but she wasn't nearly as pleasant and Shanetta had been during her check-ins. She barely acknowledged me directly. She just pulled back my covers, looked at my bandages and sheets, then threw the covers back over me. She glanced at my monitors and jotted something down on her board, then nodded her head at me before leaving. I could really tell that she didn't like her job like Shanetta did- the bitch was rude.

Realizing I wasn't going to make peace with my situation in one day, I hit the button to increase my meds and waited for sleep to ride by and pick me the fuck up.

This time, when I went to sleep, my mind was back to its usual antics. Carla was laying naked in my bed looking like I had just given her ass a real work out. I walked out of that bedroom and into another where I found Shanetta in a red lace panty and bra set looking like a million bucks.

She approached me seductively and started kissing on my neck. I let my hands roam her curves and before I knew it, we were on the bed. I was on my back and she was licking my chest making her way down.

I woke up to the feel of a cool wet cloth dragging across my forehead. When I opened my eyes, Shanetta was leaning over me.

"You were sweating pretty heavy when I came in for my first check. Are you okay?" She back away.

"Yeah, dream was a little too realistic I guess." I cleared my throat.

"I've been told the meds give you guys some crazy dreams. Want to talk about it?" She smiled sweetly.

"Ummm. Nah; but thank you for your brother-in-law's number. That was solid." I changed the subject.

"Sure, no problem." She said as she stared at my monitor and jotted down her notes. "So, who was the pretty lady?"

"That was Carla, my son's mother." I told her.

"She left out of here fast. I was still in the parking lot when she came out crying." She sat down beside my bed. "Trouble in paradise?"

"Shit, she and I haven't been a thing for about… two and a half years." Thinking about my son's age stung a little.

"Oh okay. Well, it was nice of her to come see how you're doing." She shrugged.

"I guess. Funny time for her to start thinking about my well-being." I mumbled.

"Things end badly?" Shanetta asked.

I looked into her eyes. Shit, what harm could I do by talking to her. Maybe she could give me some advice. "Yeah, things did."

"Did she cheat or you?" Shanetta asked.

"I did." I confessed. "A couple times, but we were together from young. I was going to explore my options a little. What man wouldn't?"

"A happy one. A satisfied one; but I get what you mean. You were young." She schooled me in a soft tone.

"It wasn't that I wasn't satisfied. I was just too young to be as committed as she was expecting me to be." I explained.

"What about now?" Shanetta tilted her head and her cat-eyes pierced through me.

"Now, too much has happened between us. I don't trust her the same." It was something I hadn't even told myself yet.

"Is the commitment something she still wants?"

"That depends on what day you ask her." I shook my head.

"I see. What do you want?" She asked me something I can honestly say I've never had a woman ask me before.

I paused to give it the amount of thought I felt it deserved since I might never get asked that same question again. It was a little sad that I couldn't put my thoughts into words for a response. "I don't know."

"Do you want whatever that might be with her?" Shanetta didn't skip a beat.

"No." That came easier than expected.

"Do you believe you're ready to figure out whatever that is so you can have it with the next woman?"

"Yeah, I mean what man doesn't want a good woman for himself?" I replied.

"Okay." She got up and walked toward the door.

"Where you going?" I asked.

"I'm going to let you get some rest. Besides, I have to check on my other patients. I'll be back a little later." She left my room, leaving the door cracked.

Alone with my thoughts, I couldn't help but to think about the question I couldn't answer. *Was that what Carla had been trying to point out all along? That I didn't know what I really wanted?* "Shit." I mumble under my breath.

I couldn't get back to sleep after that. I sat there thinking until the sun came up and Shanetta returned to my room.

"Something about hospitals and prison that make you think, right?" She came in like she already knew I hadn't slept.

"For sure. It's really the only time you have to sit down with your thoughts. You can't run from them or do anything to distract yourself from them." I agreed.

"So, without the distractions… are you finding clarity?" She put a bowl of soup in front of me.

"Yeah, I am." I admitted.

"You want to talk about it?" She sat down next to my bed.

"You gonna feed me this nasty ass soup?" I bargained.

"Why? Does that make it taste better?" She flirted.

"Definitely." I flirted back.

Days went by like that. With us talking and flirting; and she actually helped me realize a lot about myself. My nights were filled with deep thought and aggravation as Colinda's rudeness increased with time.

My mother came by and was surprised at my responses when she asked about what I was going to do about Carla and my son. I planned to sit Carla down and come up with some sort of coparenting agreement as soon as I was back home. I let her know that Carla and I would never be a thing romantically again and I actually felt relieved to say it out loud.

It ended up being the look in her eyes when she told me she wished she never told me about my son that sealed it for me. The sincerity in them was too much to get over. I was sure and confident that I was ready to move on. So, that's what I did. When I got home, the first thing I planned to do was take Shanetta out.

Chapter 6

Days became weeks… three weeks to be exact and physical therapy was some bullshit. The shit hurt more than it seemed to help; but according to the doctor, I couldn't leave until the physical therapist cleared me for release. I don't know how the hell that was supposed to happen when I was in more pain leaving therapy than I was going in.

Shanetta rubbed my legs down with some mint-smelling salve her grandmother had come up with in her old country house down south. I had no idea what was in it but I'll be damned if the shit didn't work.

She was spending so much time with me that it began to feel like she wasn't even working and I was loving every minute of it. We ate breakfast and lunch together, we played cards and talked and she gave me massages after therapy. I hadn't gotten a woman's full attention like this since high school. Didn't even think about how it was affecting her job because part of her job was to take care of me and I knew she was doing that very well.

It wasn't until I made a move of my own that I realized the impact her feelings for me were having on her ability to do her other work. We were talking about something deep as usual. This time, it was her feelings about gender roles in relationships. She was surprisingly traditional… so am I. In the middle of her sentence, I leaned over and kissed her -tongue and all.

Her lips were even softer than I had imagined and her tongue tasted sweet. She followed my lead and the kiss was nicer than most of the kisses

I've experienced. I took her hand and she placed the other on the side of my face. Briefly, we drifted away. We kept kissing until someone walked in.

"Oh shit." A whisper pulled us back to reality.

Shanetta jerked away and immediately dropped her head.

"What's wrong?" I asked, oblivious to the issue at hand.

The person had rushed out of the room so quickly that I didn't bother to see who it was, but Shanetta knew right away. The look on her face told me that the issue was probably major.

"That was my supervisor." She put her hands over her face.

"Okay, so what happens now?" I asked.

"I'm probably going to lose my job." She said into the palms of her hands.

I pulled her hands away from her face. "You're a nurse. There will be other work. You just have to make your move on other positions now."

She tilted her head and gave me a weak smile.

"Don't worry. We'll figure it out." I meant it as a simple comfort but the word "we'll" changed her whole mood.

She leaned in again and kissed my lips. This time, just briefly. Then she pulled away. "Okay, I'll go deal with this and I'll come back and let you know my next move regardless."

"Okay." I agreed and she left.

Before she came back another nurse, a doctor and an administrator came in to ask me questions. They weren't my bosses but I knew Shanetta would benefit from me playing my part so I told them, "I kissed her. I mean, she was caught off guard by the kissed which is why her reaction was delayed. It wasn't initiated by her though."

"So, you have feelings for Ms. Hillith?" The administrator asked.

"I mean, she has been taking such good care of me... who wouldn't? I've never had a woman take care of me like she has." That was all true.

"Are you aware that Ms. Hillith has broken some of the hospital policies?" The doctor interjected.

"How would I know that? Like I said, she hasn't done shit outside her job. I'm healing better than I expected. Shit, my insurance is paying for this, she deserves a raise." I looked them each in the eyes. "I don't see the issue. I don't work here. Plus, if I were so inclined, I'd have my lawyer look into the kind of suit I can get from the rude and rough treatment I've been getting from the day nurse."

They looked at each other. Then they all wrote something down on their clipboards.

"Okay, well thank you Mr. Lawson." The administrator said.

They all left. I was a little pissed that they actually came at me asking questions like we were high school students caught kissing in the hallway. I guess, she did break whatever rules they had for her as an employee though.

When Shanetta finally came back, she had her bag ready to go. "They're letting me go but they won't be putting the reason in my paperwork. So, I'll be able to find something at another hospital easily." She seemed relieved.

"Okay, that's good right?" I smiled.

"Yeah, that's good. I was ready to get out of here anyway. Maybe I'll start as a traveling nurse like I been saying I wanted to for a while." She shrugged.

"Look at you, got it all figured out. You coming back to see me during visiting hours?"

"Not today, I got get some shit straight first, but give me a day or two, I'll definitely come through." She smiled.

"I'm hold you to that." I told her.

"You better." She grabbed my phone and locked her number in. "Call me tonight." Then she leaned in and kissed me again.

This kiss as a little different. I could tell she had been holding back the first time. When she pulled away, I couldn't deny that I had felt something. *It was crazy; some real life movie shit.*

Chapter 7

The day finally came for me to be released. If you ask me, it didn't come soon enough. I had missed damn near a month of what was happening in the real world. One thing you find out when you go into the hospital or get locked though… the world goes on without you.

I went back home and it felt foreign at first. I had to get back used to being at my own place. My bike was completely totaled and I couldn't wait for the lawyer to get my law suit rolling. He had come to visit me the day after Shanetta got fired and he had nothing but good news for me. I was in for a nice piece of change when everything was said and done. It was just going to take some time because the company wasn't going to settle right away. I was willing to wait for the amount of money Shaub was talking, that shit was going to be a whole reset for my life and I was already planning.

Shanetta did come back to visit me two days after they let her go; and every day after that until I was released. Matter fact, I was starting to see myself keeping her fine ass. Especially, after she started cooking for me. Shorty could throw down in the kitchen.

Now that I was all healed up, I couldn't wait to see what she was working with in the bedroom; but life had some other business for me to attend to first.

My first night home, I was still coming off the effect of those meds. I thought I could go right back to my routine, but I was wrong as hell. I put me some stuffed salmon in the oven and some veggies on the stovetop and fell right to sleep.

I woke up to a full fire raging in my kitchen. The alarm was blaring, smoke was filling the house at a rate I barely had time to react to. I grabbed a few things and left out thinking I was about to lose everything.

Luckily, the area I lived in was mixed and the fire department showed up in time to get the fire put out before it hit my bedroom. I couldn't stay there, but I could grab some more closes and thank God I still had more of my belongings.

I called Shanetta and she wasted no time telling me to come stay at her spot. I let my mother know what was up and headed right over.

By the time I got there, she had the house set up for a romantic evening. Candles were lit, JoDeCi was playing softly, the smell of steak and potatoes greeted me at the door, and when I went to her bedroom... I found out she had even run me a bath. *A nigga could definitely get used to this.*

She undressed me and we both got into her huge tub. It was the most relaxing experience. She washed my body and I washed hers. The hot water damn near lulled me to sleep; but Shanetta pulled me out so we could eat.

We sat down at her table in our fluffy terrycloth towels and fed each other the delicious food she had cooked. The steak was tender, the potatoes were seasoned just right, and her steamed broccoli and cheese was perfectly cooked. Every bite had me falling harder.

Just when I didn't think the night could get any better, she led me back to her bedroom by the hand and laid me down on her bed. She warmed some oil and massaged my whole body. It was the best my body had felt since the accident.

I fell asleep under the spell of her hands. I felt her curl up beside me; so, I wrapped my arms around her. I really did miss sleeping with a warm body next to me. I had fucked plenty of bitches since Carla left, but I wasn't too fond of letting them get comfortable.

We woke up two hours later. Well, I woke up two hours later, dick harder than geometry. I slid my finger between her thighs and was pleasantly surprised to find her wet already. I slid myself inside her and stroked her awake.

The sound of her moans bounced off the walls and pushed me to keep going. The more I stroked the more she moaned. Her fat ass was soft as hell and just enough cushion to bounce me back after I plunged myself inside her.

I pulled out just long enough to turn her over and get those big thighs of hers wrapped around my waist. We kissed as I stroked and I could feel her pussy squeezing me as she came.

I kept going for another 45 minutes. *A man has to make a good first impression.* I almost forgot all about the fire at my house. She turned a bad night in a great one just like that.

The next morning, I woke up alone. She left a note saying that she had to go to work but that she had left breakfast in the microwave. I checked the time and it was 9 am. I ate the French toast, scrambled eggs, and beef sausage before jumping in the shower and heading to take care of some business myself.

The way I was feeling, I might have needed to start every day like that. I took care of my business and was setting a few new things up when my phone rang.

"Hey handsome? How's the day treating you?" Her voice was like music to my ears.

"Great thanks to you. How's it treating you?" I couldn't help smiling.

"That depends..." She said.

"On what?" I was curious.

"On whether or not you can meet me at the house for some lunch time fun." She half-whispered. "I get off in 15 minutes."

"Oh, hell yeah. I can definitely do that." I chuckled. The woman was full of surprises.

An hour later, she was peeling herself off of me, wrapped in the bed sheet. Round two had proven to be even better than the first time. I had already decided to catch a quick nap before heading back out.

"Thank you, Papa." She purred as she hopped in the shower.

"Thank YOU." I called back as the shower started.

Chapter 8

That was the beginning but it got better from there. Her sex drive was crazy. We were having sex two to three times a day – every day. I had to make her take some time off to give that kitty a rest.

She cooked everyday too. Most days, twice a day- without being asked. She kept a clean house and didn't mind cleaning up after me as far as I could tell. She was turning out to be so perfect that I was getting worried that she was too good to be true. I was waiting for the fucked-up flaw to rear its ugly head; but every day that didn't happen, I made sure to reward her once we hit the bed.

Before I knew it, two months had passed by. The owner to my place wanted to know when I was coming back home, so I had to sit her down and break the news.

I took her out to dinner; something we had started doing once a week. We sat down at this little Spanish spot and she was all smiles.

"Thank you again, baby. You know I love this spot." She reached over and took my hand.

"I know you do, baby. You don't have to thank me; but I do have something I want to talk to you about." I told her.

Her smile faded. "Oh no, what's wrong?"

"Nothings wrong. Calm down. My house is just ready for me to move back into." I took a sip of my drink.

"And you want to go?" She looked like I had just told her I was moving across the country.

"I mean... it's my place, baby. I don't want to keep crowding your space." I looked into her eyes as I spoke. "I've been loving everything you been doing. I'm not leaving you, trust me... I don't know who would be able to follow the standard you've set."

"If that's true, don't leave. I never said you were crowding my space. I don't want you to leave." Tears started to well in her eyes.

"Okay, okay. Relax. I'll just let the owner know I won't be moving back." I assured her.

She breathed deeply like she had been holding her breath and stood and leaned over the table to place kisses all over my face. "You won't regret it. I promise."

The whole thing put me on edge but I didn't let her know that. The last thing I needed was to see what level that panic attack would have gotten to. I knew then that she was in love with me, she just hadn't said it out loud yet.

Three days later, my mother asked me to come to see her at her house. So, after sending Shanetta off to work with a big smile on her face, I went over to see her.

I pulled up and an unfamiliar car was parked out front. I walked in ready to ask her about the car; but my voice got caught in my throat when a little boy came running into the living room from the kitchen.

"Hi!" He said to me before struggling to climb onto the couch.

I watched him get seated and stared closely at his face. I knew who he was without having to be told but my mother came into the living room and confirmed it for me.

"Oh, Kevin. You're here." The smile on her face was wider than I had seen it in a while.

"Hey, Ma." I mumbled but kept my eyes on the boy.

"Did you speak to him?" She asked.

"No, I..." I couldn't even say why.

"Well, don't just stand there. Come sit down." She sat down beside him.

"Gr-ma. Dank you." He said smiling up at her.

She smiled back and leaned in to kiss his forehead. "You're welcome, Kalvin!"

"Who dat?" He pointed his little chubby finger in my direction.

"That's your daddy." She told him.

He immediately got down and ran over to where I was standing. He grabbed my hand and pulled me over to the couch. "C'mon, Daddy. Sit wit me."

I could feel my mother staring at my face but I couldn't take my eyes off of him. I sat down on the couch and he climbed into my lap. I stared at him, then finally looked over at my mother.

She was still smiling. "Isn't he beautiful?"

"Yeah, he is." I agreed and wrapped my arms around my son.

He climbed up to hug me back. "Dank you, Daddy."

I looked at my mother. Neither of us said a word. Carla came walking into the living room and froze when she saw me.

"Carla, come sit down. I know you said you weren't ready but—" My mother started.

Carla cut her off. "I'll come back and get him at 8." She grabbed her purse and rushed out the door.

My mother and I both stared at the door for a few minutes.

"Don't worry, she'll come around. What's important is that you're here with him now." My mother said exactly what needed to be said.

"You're right." I agreed. "Kalvin…" I said his name for the first time.

"Yesh?" He replied happily.

"You want to hang out with Daddy today?" A lump had formed in my throat. So, I swallowed hard.

My mother reached over and touched my hand. I looked up at her and nodded that I understood her message. When I looked back down into my son's eyes, he was all smiles.

"Yesh!!" He said.

So, I took my son to the park.

Chapter 9

Eight o'clock came way too soon. We were still eating dinner at my mother's kitchen table when Carla knocked on the door. She walked in without saying a word to me. She greeted my mother and our son.

"Hey, Kal!" She bent down and kissed his forehead.

"Hey, Ma." He replied.

She flashed a weak smile at my mother. "How was he?"

"I don't know. I didn't have him until about 45 minutes ago. Ask his daddy." My mother let her know.

She looked over at me and I could tell it wasn't easy for her.

"He was good. Right, man?" I looked down at my little man.

"Yesh." She said between bites and nodded his head excitedly.

"Give me five, man. Daddy about to get out of here." I opened my palm within his reach.

He slapped my palm and jumped down from his chair. He hugged my legs tightly. I picked him up and hugged him just as tightly. I didn't want to let him ago until she came to her senses. I looked over at her. "When is he coming back, when can I see him again?"

150

She swallowed hard. "When do you want him?"

My mother smiled, clearly relieved and walked out of the kitchen.

"Next weekend." I told her. "We can go get haircuts while we're out." I offered.

"Okay." She agreed, holding her arms out for him.

"I'm serious, Carla." I held onto him.

"Me too. I'll bring him here Friday afternoon. You can keep him the whole weekend if you want." She said, her arms still waiting for me to hand him over.

"Okay." I said, still not ready to give him up.

My mother walked up behind me and gently laid her hand on my arm. I looked at her and she nodded. I understood. I kissed my son's head and handed him to his mother.

"See you Friday, man." I told him, making sure to look into his eyes. He nodded and laid his head on Carla's shoulder. I looked Carla in her eyes. "See you Friday, Carla."

She nodded her head and turned to leave. I watched her carry him out the door. Then I sat down at my mother's kitchen table and put my head down.

"I'm proud of you, Kevin." My mother rubbed my head, then leaned over me and kissed it.

"Thank you, Ma. Thank you for calling me over here to see him." I said without lifting my head.

151

I left my mother's house feeling like a new man. A father. I called Shanetta and told her how my day had gone. She was almost more excited about than I was.

"Oh, baby. I'm so happy for you. I'm so glad she changed her mind and that you got to spend some time with him. What's his name?"

"Kalvin." I said proudly.

"Okay. Does your mother know his sizes? We can pick him up some new clothes and shoes tomorrow while I'm off." She offered.

"I'll call her and find out. I'm on my way to the house. Should I stop and pick anything up on the way?"

"Nope, just bring your fine ass here. I been missing you all day."

I got home and like usual she added to the best energy of my day. She greeted me at the door with a big hug and kiss. Dinner was waiting on me and the house was clean and smelled nice. We spent the night making love and I fell asleep with a smile on my face.

I woke up to her sucking my dick. She remembered that I had to get up early and thought her throat would make the most pleasant alarm clock. I woke up to the best sensation, so I kept my eyes closed. I just ran my hands through her hair. She moaned as she sucked my dick too- like she was enjoying it just as much as I was.

We hopped in the shower together where I bent her over and came again. Then she made me a quick breakfast before kissing me goodbye and heading cheerfully out to work. Every morning was that great with Shanetta. The woman really was perfect. That's why I don't know why things went how they went next.

It wasn't that I wasn't satisfied. Like I said, her sex drive was hitting. Shit just happened. Thinking back, I can't say that I regret it; but I could have made better decisions about how I went about certain shit.

Carla called me and asked me to come to her new spot so we could talk. She sent me the address and I made my way to her. When I walked in, it was clear that booth of us had intentions on sticking to the script; but like I said before, five minutes alone…

"OH MY GOD!!! DON'T STOP!!! PLEASE, DON'T STOP!!" Carla screamed as I pulled her hair and fucked her hard from the back.

"Shut the fuck up." I mumbled. Her pussy felt like home but part of me was pissed I had been weak enough to fall back in.

"OHHH, KEVIN!!!!' She screamed as I pounded my frustration out.

I pushed her head into the mattress. I really didn't want to hear her screaming about the pleasure I was giving her. My dick might have been under her spell but everything else in me wanted that bitch crying in agony. So, I stroked harder.

The thudding of the headboard let me know that I was closer to my goal. I couldn't hear her moaning and more and the way her body was tensing up with every stroke gave me a feeling I was so grateful for. Like I was gaining my power back. Still, I stroked harder.

The bedframe gave in before she did. I had to give it to her. Carla never tapped out on my dick. No matter how I folder her ass up, no matter how rough I got… she never asked me to stop. Still, I was surprised she let me keep going after the bedframe broke.

The poor thing should have though; because I took her silence as a challenge. I stroked so hard that the sound of my pelvis crashing against hers bounced off the walls. When she finally lifted her head, she couldn't say a word, she just clasped her hands together like she was praying and cried. I kept going.

When I walked out of that house, she was laying curled up in the fetal position, rocking; and my ego was soaring. I went home to shower, then went about the business of my day. I didn't realize we hadn't talked or settled a damn thing when it came to Kalvin until I was on my way to meet Shanetta so we could shop for him.

Shanetta was so excited to be shopping for a little kid that she went overboard. We agreed to get him something to wear over the weekend he stayed with us. Then it went to us getting him a few things to keep at the house. Before I knew it, we had spent over $1,000.

I wasn't even mad though. I was glad she was excited to meet and spend time with my son. Some niggas had issues when it came to their kids with other women. So, I was counting my blessings and going with the flow.

We got home and she busied herself making space in one of the closets for his clothes. Good thing too, because Carla started calling my phone back-to-back. I had to leave the house answer after the 5th call.

"Yeah, what's up?" I answered.

"Why didn't you answer the first five times I called you?" She whined.

"I was busy. What's wrong, is Kalvin good?" I said dryly.

"Yeah, he good. I still need to talk to you though. I gotta work tomorrow but you can come back by the day after." This bitch thought she was slick.

"You can talk to me now. I got some shit to do that day." I replied.

"We have to come up with a schedule for how we're going to do this. I mean, I can use your help with him." She said.

"Alright. I'll let you know what days I can get him? He in a school or day care or something?" I asked.

"Yeah."

"Aight, text me the address." I paused to see if she had anything else to say. When she didn't, I was ready to hang up. "Let me know if he needs anything. Bye."

"Wait, Kevin." She mumbled.

"What?" I hissed.

"Why you acting like this with me?" Her voice cracked.

"We'll talk about it Friday when you come to drop my son off." I said and fought the urge to hang up. I couldn't risk her ass having another tantrum and not showing up.

"Okay." She agreed.

"Alright, bye." I hung up.

"What was that about?" Shanetta said. I had no idea how long she had been behind me but I knew I hadn't said shit out the way.

"Nothing. Just getting our schedule right for me to have Kalvin over more regularly." I told her then turned to face her.

She put her arms around me and I kissed her lips. Satisfied, she let me go. "Okay, come see how I set up his closet."

"Okay, come on." I let her lead me by the hand. All I could think was that I could not fuck Carla again. While the thought alone tripped me out, I was not about to be dealing with playing dodgeball between the two of them.

Chapter 10

Shanetta walked around the house singing Mary J Blige. "I never want to live without you baby. I want to be your lady. Your love is sooooo amazing. Never want to live without you baby..."

Now, she usually sang as she cleaned the house, but ain't it funny how music can match your life at any given moment?

"Let's make a happy hooooommmme." She kissed my lips as she passed me. Then continued singing.

I shook my head. Life wasn't not gonna catch me slipping like that. I had to make sure Carla knew what we weren't going to be doing and that Shanetta's perfect ass wouldn't have any reason to change up on me.

The rest of the flew by and the next week went by even faster. Mostly because I couldn't wait for Friday to come. Our routine went on as usual. Shanetta seemed like she had never been happier and with plans for my son to be with me regularly I was feeling the same.

By the time Friday came, I had bought Kalvin a toddler bed and set him up a space of his own in Shanetta's spare bedroom. I didn't have to ask. She saw me doing it and started helping.

Once Shanetta left for work, I headed to my mother's house. I brought with me a fresh fit for my little man to change into and planned on stopping to get him some new kicks too once I got him.

My mother let me in and she was just as excited for Kalvin come to over as I was. "Have you spoken to Carla since she left here last week?"

"Yes, I saw her on Thursday. She wanted to talk about us getting Kalvin more regularly." I told her.

"Oh, that's good, Kevin. What did you two come up with?" She sat down beside me on her couch.

"We still have some talking to do but she gave me the address to his school and put me on the list to pick him up some days. I let her know what days I would be able to keep him with me and I think I'm gonna ask to get him every other weekend. She seemed open to whatever. Said, she needed my help with him." Of course, I wasn't going to tell my mother I fucked snot out the bitch nose and walked out the house like I barely knew her; but the thought brought a big smile to my face.

"That's real good, Kevin." My mother smiled back.

We watched a little television and got so caught up in the show she had been watching that we lost track of time. When I looked up, Carla was already over and hour late.

My mother called her phone but got no answer. I didn't want to believe the bitch was tripping, so I sat there calmly for another hour. Then I decided to go to her house.

"Kevin, please be smart. This is the first time he is supposed to be away from her. Maybe she's just having some issues adjusting." My mother pleaded with my rational side.

As much as I wanted to believe that could be the case, my gut told me that her ass just wanted more of my attention so I was going to give it to her.

I pulled up in front of her house and sure enough, her car was parked right outside. I hopped out and before I could even approach the door, she came outside.

"He's sleeping." She said as if that should have been enough to appease me.

"Why the fuck didn't you bring him to my mother's house like we agreed, Carla?" I hissed.

"Why didn't you come talk to me like I asked, Kevin?" She mocked me.

I laughed. "Okay, you want to talk? Let's go inside and talk." I rushed into the house so fast that she had to backtrack to keep her distance.

"Kevin, if you hit me…" She said with fear in her eyes.

"I ain't gonna hit…at least not with my hands. Get yo stupid ass in the bedroom." I frowned,

Fear left her face and was replace by excitement. I ripped her clothes off her as soon as the bedroom door shut behind us. I knew this was all she wanted and a tiny piece of me wanted it too. I scooped her up and tossed her on the bed, then I drug her to the edge by her ankles.

She squealed and I was almost disgusted at what I was letting her bring out of me. No matter how hard I fucked her, she would not tap out. No matter how far back I pushed her legs, no matter how fast or deep I stroked her, she was enjoying it; and, in the end, I was still the weak one for giving in yet again.

Realizing this, I took a different approach. I wrapped her legs around my wasted, pinned her hands down with mine and slow stroke that pussy. I moved so slowly that even I began to feel a little hypnotized by the motions.

"Kevin, don't." She pleaded.

Ironic how she was perfectly willing to let me dog walk her ass but those slow strokes had her begging.

"Why you ain't do what you said you was gonna do? Why you ain't bring him to me like we agreed?" I said, ignoring her begging.

She got quiet. I stroked hard and she whimpered.

"You don't hear me talking to you?' I demanded.

"Yes." She whispered. "I heard you."

"So, answer me. Why you ain't bring him?" I pressed myself as far inside her as I could and held my position.

"Because..." She whispered.

"Because what, Carla? You think I'ma keep letting you play with me about my son?" I started slow stroking again, dragging myself out of her inch by inch.

"No, I'm not... I'm not playing. Kevin, please..." She was back to begging.

"Please what?" I stroked hard without warning. "Do you think I'ma keep letting you play with me?"

"No." She mumbled, trying to turn her face away.

I moved my arms in closer so her so she couldn't turn away. "This is what you wanted, right? This is what has you thinking I'm to be played with, right?" I stroke hard again without warning.

"Kevin…" She started.

I cut her off. "Shut the fuck up and take this dick. Don't play with me again like this. The next time you force me to hit you, I'ma use my hands. You understand?"

"Yes." She moaned.

"We are not a thing anymore. Do you hear me? If you want to keep getting fucked, that's fine but I got a bitch. A good one; so yo ass will be on the side. That means, you will not try my patience. I'll fuck you when I'm ready. You hear me?" I said into her ear as I stroked her body like I loved her. "This is the only feeling you will get out of me from today forward. Ain't no love in this shit. You get me?"

A single tear slid from each of her eyes. "Yes."

"Good, now cum on this dick." I demanded.

Thirty minutes later, Kalvin and I were on our way.

Chapter 11

I didn't have to worry about Carla for a few months after that. I guess I bruised her ego and she didn't want to have to play the side chick. Maybe I could have gone easier on her, but my point was made. She gave me no grief at all when it came to getting Kalvin. Matter fact, she even let Shanetta pick him up from her a few times.

My mother and I were both developing great relationships with Kalvin. Shanetta and I were growing closer as time passed and I had finally gotten Carla off my mind full-time. Things were going so smoothly that I could feel the fumble coming a mile away.

A year had passed and despite the fact that the trucking company still wasn't ready to settle my case, business was moving as usual. Carla called me over to talk for the first time in months. I almost believed she actually did want to talk this time.

I pulled up to her house and was surprised at how nice she was acting. She met me at the door, offered to cook for me and handed me a beer before we sat down in her living room.

"What's up, Carla. I have some business to attend to. I don't have time for your head games." I told her.

"No games, Kevin. I just wanted to thank you for how much you've been helping me with Kalvin. When I left you, I didn't expect to see this type of change in you for a long time. I should have given you more credit."

I just stared at her for a few seconds. I couldn't tell what type of time she was on.

"Kevin, I'm serious. I owe you an apology. I don't want the decision I made out of fear and frustration held over my head any longer."

She was definitely on some bullshit; I just didn't know what or why yet. "What the fuck you got going on, Carla?" I eyed her.

"I've been thinking and I want to try and work on us for Kalvin. He deserves to have both of us. As a family."

I couldn't believe my ears. This was the complete opposite of what she was saying that night she stormed out of my house. "I don't have time for this. Where is my son?"

"He's at my sister's house. I really just called you here to talk about this. You really don't want to give us a chance?" She looked up at me like she was a lost puppy.

"No. I don't." I said dryly. "You know I'm with Shanetta. Besides, why you want this now all of a sudden? I remember you saying I hadn't changed and you were sorry you even told me about Kalvin." The memory put a bad taste in my mouth.

"But you have changed. That's what I'm saying." She approached me.

I found myself backing away from her. She was right; I had changed. Just not in the way she was talking about. It was the first time since we met way back in high school freshman year that I could control my hormones around her. My dick didn't even twitch in her presence. I was deep in thought, trying to figure out if that was good or bad when she made her move.

"Kevin, I know you ain't let this woman come in and undo what we've had forever. I know you still love me; you're just upset at what I did." She leaned in and pressed her soft ass lips to my neck. "You have every right to be." She slid her tongue from my neck to my earlobe. "…but it's time for us to start making up." She kissed my earlobe.

I didn't have to question whether or not my lack of reaction to her was growth or not anymore because my body was overreacting. The head of my dick was throbbing like the hurt toe of a cartoon character. I looked Carla in her face. "Why now, Carla? Wasn't that you saying that you ain't want nothing to do with me?"

"Baby, I was just scared you wouldn't be the father I needed you to be. I was scared we wouldn't be what Kalvin deserved." Her breath tickled my neck.

"And what makes you so sure that's not the case now?" I asked, trying to keep my hands to myself.

"Because…" She pressed her lips to my neck again; only this time, she sucked on it and twirled the tip of her tongue.

I felt a knot form in my stomach. I kept thinking about how weak I felt giving into to this woman the last time. So, I leaned away from her. "Carla, I'm not fucking you and I'm not fucking with you. I don't need a bitch that's gonna fold on me. I'ma do what I gotta do for Kalvin; but we done."

She frowned. "Nah, we ain't done. You just mad. So, what I gotta do to apologize?" She scooted closer to me and kissed the side of my face. Then she kissed the side of my mouth. Then she kissed my lips. "I want to make it up to you. I know I fucked up big; but I want to make it up to you. Baby, let me make it up. Please?"

I tried my hardest not to kiss her back; but her lips were so soft. She slipped her tongue between my lips and the taste jolly ranchers brought back high school memories. She always sucked a jolly rancher before kissing me.

I sucked her tongue and she moaned a little into my mouth. I had to admit this woman was my weakness because that moan sent me over the edge. I started taking her clothes off and she started taking off mine. She didn't even bother to wear panties or a bra. She just knew I was gonna fall for the bullshit.

We were all over each other. I sucked on her nipples and licked on her stomach; she kissed from my neck down to that crease on my hips. She bit that spot and I had to stop myself from cumming. She giggled, knowing she had me right where she wanted then. Then she sucked the head of my dick into her mouth without using her hands.

She didn't lie about wanting to make that bullshit up to me. She sucked my dick like my pleasure was the only thing that could save her life. I ended up with both hands behind her head, fucking her face. I stopped her as soon as I felt myself ready to cum. She wasn't getting off that easy.

I laid her back on the arm of the couch with her ass hanging off and put her ankles on my shoulders. Just as I was sliding into her wetness, I hear the front door slam. I looked up and Shanetta was standing there with tears in her eyes.

Chapter 12

I snatched myself out of Carla, who was now laughing so hard that she was holding her stomach. Holding my dick in one hand, I approached Shanetta, but she took off running out the door. So, I turned to Carla. *This shit was clearly a set up because why the fuck was the door open?*

"What the fuck was that, Carla?" I snapped. "Why the fuck was the door open? How she know to come here to find me?"

"I told her to come. She needed to know that she can't stop this train. This is a forever thing. We for-lifers, baby. You had her thinking she could keep you from me; so, I had to let her know."

I wanted to slap the bitch. *Two months ago, she ain't want me; now we "for-lifers".* I rushed to put my clothes.

"Where the fuck you going? I know you're not about to run after that bitch. You just let me walk out your door when I was ready to leave you." She looked disgusted.

I pulled my shirt over my head. "You ain't her." I said it knowing it would hurt her feelings. Being honest with myself, I knew I still had some feelings left for Carla; but she wasn't the same person I fell for back in the day. This petty shit was new.

"That's how you feel?" She stood in front of me, still completely naked.

I looked at her, her whole body, like I might not see it again. Then I walked out the door and hopped in my car. I had to find Shanetta and apologize.

I had no idea where Shanetta had run off to. I checked the house, but she wasn't there. I called her phone back-to-back but she wasn't answering. I left messages and texted her, but got no response. I even stopped by her best friend's house and her job. Only after my third trip to the house did I find her pulling up.

I pulled up behind her so she couldn't leave. Then I hopped out the car and ran to her driver's side door. She wouldn't open the door.

"Shanetta. Please hear me out. I didn't go over there planning to fuck her. I know I was weak, but you gotta believe me. I don't want her. That just happened." I pled my case.

"How the fuck am I supposed to believe it won't just happen again? Or that it won't keep happening?" Her eyes were red and puffy from crying.

I reached into her window and unlocked her door. Then I opened it and got down on my knees beside her. "Because…" I had a choice to make but it wasn't a hard one. Shanetta was a good woman. So, I told her, "I love you. I'll never do anything like this again. I don't want to hurt you. Believe me." I wiped a tear from her check and leaned in and put kisses all over her face.

Eventually, she started to kiss me back. "What the fuck, Kevin? She called me to stop by. Texted me saying the door would be open. She was nice before but never that welcoming; so, I should have known it was something. Still, how could you do that? Don't I satisfy you?" She started crying all over again.

"Yes; this had nothing to do with how I feel about you. I love fucking you, Shanetta. I just…" I paused.

167

"What? Tell me!" She demanded.

"Nothing. No excuse. It will never happen again. I swear." I took her by the hand and we went into the house. I spent the rest of the night making Shanetta feel like no one else mattered.

The next morning, I asked her to take off of work but she declined. I think she wanted the time away from me to think. I had to respect that. Part of me wanted to go over to Carla's to set that petty bitch straight; but more of me knew I needed to stay away from there for a while. I couldn't tell Shanetta, but I knew she was my addiction and that I might always be a little weak for her.

It was something I never really had to think about when we were together but definitely something I was growing to hate about myself the longer we were apart. No bitch deserved that power over me. Especially not Carla after the shitty stunts she had been pulling. I had to figure out how to break her spell over me.

I hit the gym. With no bike, I had to do something to clear my head. There was still a chance that Shanetta wanted out; but after all her bullshit there was no way I'd go back to Carla. Four miles on the treadmill and two hours on the heavy weights didn't do shit. I was still lost in my thoughts. I needed a new bike.

I went back to the house, showered and laid down. Before I knew it, I dozed off. I don't know how long I was out; but I woke up to Shanetta kissing my face. I immediately took her into my arms and pulled her into bed with me. She stripped down and fell asleep on my chest.

It was 3 am when we woke up again. I was lying there staring at the ceiling when she just started talking. "She told me that you will always love her; that nothing I can do will make you love me the way you love her. Is that true?"

"No. I don't love her like that anymore. I had a moment of weakness; I'm in love with you." I told her.

"A weak moment. What's going to stop you from having another one?" It was a legitimate question.

"I hate myself for it. The last thing I ever wanted to do was hurt you. I think you're perfect in so many ways, that's an 'L' I'm not willing to take." I confessed.

"You really think that?" She sat up to look me in the eyes.

"Definitely." I leaned over and kissed her lips.

The kiss got deeper and before she knew it, I was going deep myself. I was really relieved to know she wasn't going anywhere. Still, I had to figure out what to do about Carla.

Shanetta

Carla had another thing coming if she thought I was just going to let her have him that easily. I hadn't been that happy with a man in years. There was no way I was letting her have him. That shady bitch had me fucked up.

Hearing Keno say he was in love with me, let me know the relationship was worth fighting for. Shit, I seen bitches stay with niggas who did way worse than fucking his baby mother. I had to be real with myself though. *If he kept fucking her, would I stay? If this wasn't the last time this shit occurred, would I be content sharing him with her occasionally? Hell yes! A good man is hard to find.*

Carla

I was furious when Keno left my house. *What the fuck did he mean I wasn't her? Who the fuck was this new bitch really, to have him changing up on me after so long?*

I sat on my couch for a minute, wondering if he was for real and what I could do to change that. Shanetta and I had exchanged numbers when Kalvin started going over to her house. I acted cool but I was never really okay with the shit. I just assumed the bitch was temporary. I guess I thought wrong.

I called his phone a couple of times but he didn't answer. When 10 o'clock came around, I was pissed. He really chased after her and wasn't coming back. By four am, I had already bounced between crying to throwing shit and back. *What did she have that I didn't?*

Chapter 13

I had no idea at the time, but Carla wasn't ready to just give up on our relationship or her hopes for us to be a family. If I had time to cater to her bullshit, I probably could have had a little more control in the situation; but I was busy trying to get over her so I could move the fuck on.

I had my mother picking Kalvin up for me. It had been three weeks without incident but I knew better than to think shit was sweet. I had to keep my distance until I was sure we had a clear understanding.

It was a Wednesday when I realized Carla might have never been who I thought she was. The fucked-up thing about it was that it turned me on a little. A lot, if I'm being honest. Yeah, it was wrong, but having a woman go to such lengths just to be me with definitely stroked the ego.

Shanetta and I started our day out with sex. Her sex drive had increased after I told her I love her. We were up to three times a day, every day. A nigga was getting all the pussy and throat he could stand. I ended every night completely drained and smiling. That morning, she rode me like I was her favorite ride; then made me French toast, eggs sunny side up, and couple of strips of turkey bacon before kissing me goodbye and heading to work.

I ate my breakfast, took a couple of business calls, and got ready to hit the gym. I had a meeting with my lawyer that afternoon; so, I brought a change of clothes and planned to change and head straight to his office afterward.

I did my usual workout on the treadmill and heavy weights. Then I went to the massage chairs to wind down. I had only just added this to my gym regiment. So, she had to be following me to know I would go in there. I closed my eyes as I was enjoying the massage.

I felt the warm, wet sensation of a tongue glide from my belly button up to the middle of my chest. I opened my eyes and found Carla hovering over me. My first reaction was to grab her and push her away. I sat up. "What the fuck are you doing, Carla?" She put her finger over my lips and mushed me back in a laying position. I sat up again. She wasn't gonna catch me slipping twice. "Hell no. Get the fuck out of here."

"You want to stay with her, I don't care. You love her, so fucking what. I deserve to have what I want after everything I've been through with you. I want you." She whispered aggressively.

"Carla, I'm not…" I started to say.

She cut me off. "You love me. I know you still love me; and you can love us both. I won't make it difficult. Just give me what I want when I ask."

Her offer sounded too good to turn down; but I wasn't about to fall for the okey-doke. "How do I know you ain't call Shanetta and let her know it was going down again? How do I know you won't get back on your bullshit once you get the pipe? Shit, how I know you won't up and disappear with my son if shit don't go your way?"

"All I'm asking for is consistent dick and help with Kalvin. You're already on your shit with Kal. Just fuck me regularly and we good. I swear, I won't cause any friction." She said as she straddled me.

Another gym patron walked into the massage room, but backed out when they saw the comprising position Carla had me in. "Pardon me, my guy. Do your thing. Maybe lock the door though."

I looked at Carla and she got up and locked the door. "So? Are we doing this?"

I thought about it for a second. She was definitely looking good; and even though I was getting more than enough at home. Carla's pussy was too good to refuse if it wouldn't cause me any issues. "The first sign of problems out of you and I'm cutting you off."

She smiled devilishly and began stripping. The more clothes she took off, the harder my dick got. I set the massage chair for 30 minutes and pulled my dick out. Then I laid back and let her drive.

Thirty minutes later, I walked out of there smiling. I was ten minutes late to meet my lawyer; but I gave him a call and took a quick shower. When I walked out of the gym, Carla was nowhere in sight. *Maybe this thing could work out after all.*

Carla

I still don't believe Keno will stay with Shanetta. He just hasn't come to his senses yet. Regardless, I learned something about myself. Sneak-dickin is more exciting to me than being in a relationship. I get all the benefit without any of the headache or heartache. My pussy was throbbing for two hours from the pounding that muthafucka gave me at that gym. I had to go home and soak in a hot bath. You know what though, the peace of not being the one waiting at home while he was out cheating almost made me want them to stay together.

Shanetta

Sitting in the bathroom, shocked to the point of not being able to move. Every negative thought was going through my mind. I ain't have time for no baby. Shit, Keno was only a minute off dicking down Kalvin's mother. We were nowhere near stable enough to bring a baby into the equation.

I dropped my head, knowing I had to make that appointment. I had always been the woman downing my friends for getting themselves knocked up and having to lay on that table. *Now look at me.*

***

I went home feeling myself. I mean on top of the world. Shanetta had dinner going as usual. The house was clean and welcoming. She greeted me with a kiss and I greeted her back with a tap on her fat ass.

She seemed a little off but I brushed it off as me being a little paranoid after my extracurricular activities. So, I wasn't going to press it and give my guilty self away. I showered and we ate. Then we laid together and just cuddled- something we hadn't done in months because her sexual appetite was just that lit. It was nice.

Chapter 14

Shanetta was still acting off the next morning. She didn't wake me up for sex; and even though she made breakfast, she wasn't her usual cheery self. "Are you okay?" I asked her for the third time since we woke up.

"Yeah." She said and offered a weak smile.

"Come on; tell me what's up. You gotta know I know you better than that." I pressed.

She looked like she was actually thinking about whether she should tell me what was going on or not. Then my phone rang with a business call I was expecting. So, she kissed me goodbye and left for work. I made a mental to note to bring it back up later that night and went about my day.

The day went by quickly, with everything going my way effortlessly. I was still singing the song that was playing on the ride home when I got a call from her. "Hey, baby." I answered. Realizing, she wasn't home as I walked in. "Where are you?"

She was quiet at first. When she finally spoke, she sounded like she was in pain. "I need you to come get me."

"What's wrong? Where are you?" I said already heading back out to my car.

"I'm at Havenwood." She mumbled.

I just knew I heard her wrong. "Where?"

"Havenwood." She repeated herself.

"What the fuck are you doing there?" I sat behind the wheel with my door still open, hoping she wasn't saying what the fuck I thought she was saying.

"I made an appointment… but I couldn't go through with it. I left my car at work and my nerves are a wreck. Please, just come get me." She started crying.

"So, you're pregnant.?" I asked the obvious.

"Yes." She got quiet. "If you don't want me to keep it, you'll have to come with me. I can't do this alone."

"I'm on my way" was all I said. We stayed on the phone but didn't say a word to each other until I got there.

It was a twenty-minute ride. All I kept thinking was how many times I had asked her to tell me what was wrong. I had given her so many opportunities to tell me. I pulled up in front of the abortion clinic. "I'm outside. Do I need to come in and get you?" I asked her, only half believing she hadn't gone through with it.

"No. I told you, I didn't go through with it. I'm coming now." She mumbled.

I got out and opened her door for her as usual. She went out her way to look me in the eyes but I avoided locking eyes with her. I waited for her to get in and closed her door. Then walked around to the driver's side and decided what approach to take. When I got in, I said my peace right away. "Are you still pregnant?"

"Yes."

"I don't know why you didn't want to talk about this with me before you decided to make this appointment. I thought we had a better understanding than that. Still, I'm not mad. We just need to talk when we get home."

"I want to keep it." She blurted out. "I know you're going through this mess with Carla and maybe this isn't the best time for this to be happening; but it happened. I want it."

"You sure? You didn't want it this morning when you came here; or whatever day you made the appointment." I side-eyed her.

"I know, I'm sorry but when I got to this place, I couldn't do it. I want our baby." She seemed to be pleading with me.

I had to really think about the situation. A year and a half ago, I didn't have any kids; now I had two and two baby mothers. Carla was for sure going to freak the fuck out when she found out. Then I would have to worry about if she told Shanetta we were back fucking. The shit was mess.

"Let's talk about it when we get home." I told her.

Shanetta

The whole car ride home, neither of us said a word. I didn't know how to take that. I couldn't tell what he was thinking. Nothing he had said told me whether he was mad about the fact that I made the appointment or that I was pregnant.

When we got home, I was pleasantly surprised when he pulled me into a hug and said, "I'm glad you didn't go through with that shit. I want you to keep it. That might be my girl."

I was so happy to hear it, I started to cry all over again. "Thank you. I was so scared you would say it would be too much with the whole situation with Carla." I confessed.

"Yeah; let me worry about all that. You just make sure not to stress my baby out." He rubbed my stomach, kissed my lips, and walked off.

"Come get in the shower, we can order something to eat." He called over his shoulder.

I followed him like a puppy.

Carla

Never in a million years did I expect Shanetta's sneaky ass to one up me. I let her know I wasn't going nowhere and the bitch got pregnant. I couldn't believe my fucking ears when Keno called me to break the news. His ass was sounding tough but really, he was begging me not to let the cat out the bag about us. I didn't give a fuck if the bitch gave birth to a whole litter of his kids. Since she wanted to share, fuck it... he was ours. Long as I got what I wanted out the deal, I could care less. Let her dumb ass sign up to be the one at home crying. It was nice that it wouldn't be me for a change.

Chapter 15

Carla took the news about the baby way better than I expected. She laughed and said, "Maybe Shanetta will leave you on her own when she's the one getting cheated on. I know I was pushed to that point multiple times. We gonna see if Shanetta is as strong as you think now."

I had to admit, she was right about that. If I had learned anything from my situation with Carla, it was that you don't really know your woman until she gets pregnant by you. Carla had been everything I wanted for years. I shot up her club one time, made Kalvin, and now I barely know the bitch.

So, that got me to thinking on what I needed to do to make the whole situation, Carla included, go my way. I didn't want any hiccups, drama, or misunderstandings. Carla seemed like she was content playing the sidelines and if I could have them both, I'd never have to look at another woman again. *I swear my intention was to be faithful to both of them. I was making family plans for the five of us; me, Shanetta, Carla, Kalvin and whoever this little bun in the oven turned out to be… but you know, shit never goes how it's supposed to.*

Shit was going smooth at first. I was going to every appointment with Shanetta, spending time with Kalvin and moms, and dickin Carla whenever she asked. She wasn't even asking at times she knew it would be inconvenient for me. I was starting to think I could get used to life the way it was.

I had been bragging to the boys about my "sister-wives"; and they kept warning me that the situation was going to crumble when I least expected it. I just thought I had everything under control.

One late afternoon, I was at Carla's enjoying the feel of her mouth when Shanetta called. No big deal; I had taken her calls before while fucking Carla. She was really playing her roll as long as it meant she would cum enough times before I left. This call was different though. When I answered, Shanetta was crying to the point that I barely understood her.

"Slow down. What's wrong?" I asked her.

"I'm at the hospital. Something's wrong with the baby." She said between sobs. "Come now."

"I'm on my way." I told her and hung up.

"I know you're not leaving. You haven't even touched my pussy. You just got here." Carla sucked her teeth and got up from her kneeling position in front of me.

"Something's wrong with the baby. I have to meet her at the hospital." I told her as I zipped my pants.

"Ain't shit wrong with that girl. She probably just wants some attention. Make me cum before you leave." She pulled off her shorts and laid on the couch with her legs spread.

"I got you when I get back." I told her.

"Who knows when the fuck that will be." She hissed.

"Carla, don't start your bullshit. This is serious. I'll be back." I told her. "I'll make you cum however you want me to when I get back. Fuck with me on this."

"Fine. Bye." She walked away. "Lock my door behind you."

I rushed out, using my key to lock her door and sped all the way to the hospital but it was already too late. Shanetta's doctor said they couldn't find the baby's heartbeat and they wanted to induce her labor.

At five months, one week, and two days, Shanetta gave birth to our daughter who was still born. She cried the rest of the night. Of course, I stayed and held her.

Holding my daughter's lifeless body was a different kind of pain. I kissed her little hands and held Shanetta in my arms as she held her and said her own goodbyes. Carla kept blowing my phone up. I eventually turned it off.

Carla

I didn't give a fuck what happened to that bitch's baby. Me and Keno had a deal; *I got what I want, or Shanetta would find out what she didn't know.* He really thought I was playing with him. Well, he was about to find out who got the last laugh around that muthafucka.

I grabbed my phone and pulled up the ammo I had been gathering just in case some bullshit like that happened. When I hit send, I laughed myself to tears. Poor Shanetta was in for some eye-opening truth that day; and Keno was just going to have to deal with the consequences.

Shanetta

I woke up in the middle of the night and smiled when I realized Keno was still holding me. I kissed his hand then slowly slipped from his embrace. I initially was just going to the bathroom but I decided to check my phone while I was up.

You ever find something out that changes everything? Ever discover something you wish you could un-know? I wished I had never checked my phone. At least not until we left the hospital. My heart got broken twice that day.

I had never been pregnant before. Losing my daughter was still a large aching hole in my heart when I realized Keno had been cheating on me for what looked like my entire pregnancy. I couldn't respond to her texts, all I could do was drop to my knees. I literally had nothing left.

Chapter 16

I woke up to Shanetta slapping me in the face. I almost slapped her ass back. Women think that shit is cool; but her ass almost found out first-hand what that shit gets you.

"What the fuck?" I barked at her.

"YOU TELL ME!!" She threw her phone at me.

I fumbled it a couple of times before I caught it in the palms of my hands and looked at the screen. It was a picture of me laying on Carla's chest fast asleep. Drooling. I'll admit it, in the beginning I was sloppy. I was catching naps there if the sessions got good, buying her shit like I used to, and even taking her out to eat occasionally. I got too comfortable once I knew she was sticking to the agreement.

"Shanetta, I…" I got up and walked toward her.

"Shut the fuck up, Kevin. I knew it possible that you were still fucking that bitch." She backed away from me as she whispered. "I want to know why she felt the need to share this shit with me the morning after our baby died. Was you with her when I called you? Is that the shit you do every time I'm not around?" She shot out rapid-fire questions.

"Yes, I was; but no that's not all I do when you're not around." I ain't have the patience to lie. "Yes, I've been fucking her; but I was never going to leave you for her."

"Oh, you were just going to keep fucking us both?"

I didn't know what to say. I felt like the "yes" I wanted to give her would have made things worse.

"Okay." She caught me completely off guard with that response. "I don't have the energy to fight you on this. Maybe later, I'll move on; but for now, just do whatever you want." She climbed into the hospital bed and turned her back to me.

I put my arm around her, expecting her to push me off of her, but she didn't. The shit felt worse than arguing.

Carla

Keno said he thought Shanetta was depressed or something after I sent those texts. If you ask me, that was what the bitch gets. I let her know twice what this was and she decided to stay. Maybe her ass just had low self-esteem. Who the fuck is okay with knowing they're being cheated on? Unless she cheating back. Hell, for all we know that baby might not have even been Kevin's.

Either way, it worked out for me. For the next two months, I was getting more dick than I could stand. I was actually going to tell him I needed a break when it happened. Shanetta surprised me with that one.

185

****

I never saw the shit coming. This was some shit I saw Carla's shady ass doing first. Two months after our daughter passed, things were still strained but getting closer to normal. Shanetta was still healing so I was at Carla's damn near ever other day. I was still coming home to home-cooked meals, a clean house, and cuddles like everything was cool. So, in my mind… it was.

One night, even though I was late coming in, she wasn't home when I got there. The only other time this had happened, her ass ended up at Havenwood. I called her phone and got no answer. So, naturally, I was suspicious.

I went to her job and her car was still parked in her space, but when I went inside, they told me she had already left. I called her again and she still didn't pick up. So, parked where I could watch her car and waited.

An hour and a half later, a car pulled up behind hers. Some guy got out of the driver's side and opened the passenger door. She got out wearing a tightly fitted dress and heels. I hopped out and was standing next to them in no time.

"Oh my God, Keno. What are you doing here?" Surprise was all over her face.

"No, what the fuck are you doing here? Dressed like this; and with this nigga." I stared her friend down.

"Who is this?" He had the balls to ask.

"Who the fuck are you?" I barked back.

"Kevin, it's not what it looks like…" She started explaining.

"Really? Because it looks like this muthafucka just took you out on a date." I said through a clenched jaw.

"Oh, this is your man?" The nigga interjected. "Oh, homie. I ain't mean to step on your toes. I ain't know she was taken." He backed away and got into his car, pulling off without saying another word to her.

"So, you went out on a fucking date?" I glared at her in disgust.

"Don't do that. You been fucking Carla every damn day. I ain't fuck him; but yes, I let him take me out to eat." She confessed.

"Get in the car. I'ma see your ass at the house." I gave her my back.

When we got in the house and I got a better look at her, I got even more mad. She had done her make up and everything to go see this muthafucka. "Lucky man, you was looking good. Where he take you?" I said sarcastically. She just stared at me like I hadn't just asked her a question. "I gotta ask you again? Or are you saying it's none of my business?"

"We went to Benihana's." She mumbled.

"Oh, he cut a check. He tryna get in where he fit in for real." I said, still frowning at how beautiful she looked.

"Like I said, it was just dinner." She sighed.

"Where you meet him?" I had to know.

"His mother was one of my patients a couple of weeks back." She admitted.

"So, y'all been talking for a while. How many is a couple? Was this the first date? Or did he start with lunch?"

"Keno…" She sighed heavily, probably realizing it was best to answer my questions. "Three weeks. His mother was my patient for a week three weeks ago. On the day she was released, he asked me for my number. I gave it to him, thinking 'fuck it, you had Carla'. We texted for a while. Then, yesterday, he asked me out. I turned on your location on your phone, so I knew every time you were at Carla's. Every time; and you know how many times that was. So, I figured one date would hurt." She plopped down on the couch.

I sat down next to her; but didn't say a word.

"Is this what's it's gonna be? Me, you and her? Because if this is it, I want out." She said what I already felt was coming.

I thought about it. She was asking me to give up Carla for good. Could I really do that? Was fucking Carla worth losing Shanetta? I had to give her an answer… so I lied. "Nah. This is not it. I don't want you going on anymore dates. I'll cut her off."

"I wish I could believe you." She shook her head.

"Shit, you said you knew every time I was at her spot, right? So won't you know?" I looked over at her.

Her eyes looked exhausted. Like the kind of tired no amount of sleep can do anything to help. I felt like shit because I knew losing the baby had done something to her.

"I guess we'll see then." She got up.

"You gonna cut that nigga off?" I followed her.

"Like I said, I guess we'll see." She went into the bedroom.

188

I ain't like the sound of that shit. I was on her heels. "What the fuck is that supposed to mean?"

"I said what I said." She walked into the bathroom and started running herself a bath. The lack of 'give-a-fuck' in her voice told me she would definitely leave me if I got caught up with Carla again.

"I'll cut the shit off with Carla in the morning." I said.

"Enjoy the last time… if that's really the case." She said like she didn't really care.

"Enjoy your bath." I went back into the living room to think. It would have been the perfect time to ride my bike.

Chapter 17

Carla

I had just gotten out of the tub. I usually soaked my body before Keno came over for a session. When I heard his key in the door, I got excited as usual; but when he walked in, I knew he was about to tell me some bullshit. "I don't even want to hear it."

He sat down on my couch like the weight of the world was on his shoulders. "Come sit with me." He patted the cushion beside him.

I sat down beside him. "What now?"

"Today has to be the last time." He said it without looking at me.

"Not this shit again. We already talked about this." I wasn't going for it.

"I know; but I'm serious. This is it. So, let's make it good." He started taking off his clothes.

The way he said it, the sadness in his voice almost made me believe him; but my ego told me 'Ain't no way he would really just walk away'. I took off my robe and he led me by the hand to my bedroom.

Them slow strokes had me moaning and crying, emotions all over the place. He was really leaving me... for that bitch. *What was it about her? What the fuck did she have that I didn't?*

When he kissed me on my forehead before he got up out of my bed and got dressed, I knew he was for real.

"Carla, this can't affect shit we do with and for Kalvin. He deserves both of us. Please don't make that difficult." He looked me in my eyes.

I nodded that I understood and he walked out of my bedroom. He didn't go to the bathroom to shower. I heard the door slam and the shit broke my heart.

****

I left Carla's house feeling sick to my stomach. For one, I couldn't believe how much it was hurting to stop fucking that girl. Even after everything she had put me through when it came to Kalvin and Shanetta, it was still hard to cut things off. Secondly, I felt disgusted with myself knowing I was still so weak for her. I would even have to change how I moved when it came to Kalvin; I couldn't risk giving in because I knew she would try me.

Watching her house disappear in my rearview mirror, I knew I wouldn't see that house again, I tried my best to leave everything I enjoyed about her behind.

Shanetta

I decided to take the day off. I wanted to see if he really went through with trying to cut Carla off. I knew the shit would be hard for him; but seeing him come in the house clearly broken up about it cut me to the core. He obviously still loved that woman. That kind of shit, I couldn't compete with. She was always going to be an issue if I stayed... it was like the bitch was his drug.

I greeted him with a kiss on the cheek, he flashed me a weak smile and kissed my face but there was barely any feeling to it. I stayed in the living room. I could tell he needed some space and time to himself. It hurt me to give it to him, but the fact that he was willing to put himself through that kind of struggle for me gave me a little hope.

He stayed in the shower for an hour. I had to keep stopping myself from going in there. The situation had me feeling like I was walking on egg shells. *How the fuck did Carla's shady ass get a nigga to fall so deep for her? What was it about her?*

****

I kept saying to myself, "This bitch had better be worth feeling this. One hint of some bullshit and I would kill her ass. I knew Carla would never look at me the same for really choosing Shanetta over her. I had slammed the door on the possibility of us being the family she had wanted for so long. The reason she stayed while I drug her through all the shit I put her through... the cheating and fighting, the arguments and disrespect.

I had already made my choice; but the jury was still out on how good of a decision it was.

Chapter 18

A few weeks passed and I was starting to feel like I was getting over my "withdrawal". I wasn't having anymore wet dreams about Carla and sex with Shanetta was finally getting back to normal. I struggled at first. I would barely fuck Shanetta well enough to make sure she came... not even cumming myself sometimes. Then I would have vivid ass dreams about Carla and wake up with cum leaking out of my dick. I knew that shit fucked Shanetta up; but she rocked with a nigga... not even complaining about it once.

With shit finally getting closer to our normal, we had sex and started our day with breakfast as usual. Then she went off to work and I went for a meeting with my lawyer. The trucking company was finally ready to settle. It had been two whole years.

I got showered and dressed and headed to Mr. Shaub's office. He greeted me with a big smile and I knew right away I was in for good news. We shook hands and he closed his office door behind me.

Shanetta

My day at work started off hectic. I had a dementia patient who was physically abusive. I got hit in the face while I was wiping her shitty ass and had to dodge a few kicks too. After that, the head nurse for my department pulled me aside and let me know another department was short staff and I would have to float for the rest of my shift. That was a nurse's nightmare; and just my luck, I ended up in labor and delivery.

I assisted in the deliver of three of the sweetest babies I had every experienced and by lunch I was in full panic attack mode. My heart ached because I kept seeing my daughter's face in my head and I couldn't even go home because I didn't want to have to see the sad look on his face. He was getting better about losing Carla but the fact that he was grieving the loss was still in his eyes.

I sat in one of the break areas and took some deep breaths. I had to pull my shit together. I had been having the attacks since Brianna's birth but I thought I was getting a handle on them. Seeing those babies put me back at square one. My phone rang and his voice immediately put me at ease.

"Something said you needed to be checked on."

Carla

The last thing I was expected was to get a call from Kalvin's school. I went racing down there as soon as they told me. I shot Kevin a text and he met me there. This was not going to become a regular thing.

"Carla, you gotta relax. Boys fight. I'm proud of him for not backing down. What you want him to let people beat up on him?" He chuckled, clearly not seeing where I was coming from.

"Keno, it's deeper than that. Yes, boys do fight; but I'm not about to be up at every school he goes to because he got your attitude and temper. You need to explain to him that he doesn't always have to use his hands." I explained.

"Okay, okay. You're right. I'll talk to him. Let me take him with me. Does he need anything." He flashed a smile and I had to look away.

"Nah, he don't need nothing. Just bring him home so he can get to bed on time." When I finally looked his way again, we locked eyes.

"No problem." He said.

We went our separate ways. I kissed my son goodbye and headed to the nail salon. I was I desperate need of some pampering and self-love.

Chapter 19

Hanging with Kalvin was always cool. He was a cool little dude. Especially, since he started preschool. "So, what happened man?" I asked him.

"Daddy, he hit me." He told me what I already knew.

Whether or not he had my temper was yet to be confirmed. I didn't know why Carla was trippin, he was a good kid... but I had taught him not to let any of those kids put their hands on him.

"So, what you do?"

He smiled wide, proud of himself. "I hit him back hard. Just like you told me."

"Good. That's my boy." I rubbed his head.

"So, you not mad?" He looked up at me.

"Nah, man. You are supposed to fight back. Just don't be in there starting no trouble." I warned him.

"Mommy's mad." He looked out the window.

"She'll be alright. You did good, you hear me?" I assured him.

"Yes." He nodded.

"You hungry? You want get something to eat?" I asked.

"Yeah." His energy went from somewhat sad back to hype.

"Aight come on. Let's go to our spot. Then we can go to the barbershop and get that nappy head cut." I joked.

He rubbed his head and shot me a look. I had to laugh, *maybe he did have my temper.*

We got burgers and fries at this spot I always took him to when we hung out. Then we got hit the barbershop and I got both of our heads cut. After that, I took him to the mall. We got ice cream and went into a toy store.

"Daddy, I like when we together." He told me between licks of his ice cream cone.

"I like it too." I let him know.

"I wish we could do it more. Why you don't come to our house no more?" He asked innocently, but it hit me hard.

"Mommy and I need some time apart. So, we can work together better and take better care of you." I told him the first thing that came to my head.

"But you do gooder when you're together." He said, getting ice cream all over his face.

I didn't have a response. I just kept hearing Carla's voice in my head, *He deserves a family.* I wiped his face and we sat there and finished our ice cream in silence. Then I took him into a shoe store. I let him try on six pairs of shoes and bought all of them. I got three pairs for myself and a pair for Shanetta.

"You gonna get Mommy some shoes too?" He asked me when I told him the 'girlie' pair was for his stepmother.

"You think I should?" I asked him.

"Daddies is supposed to buy mommies stuff. My friend Michael said his daddy buys his mommy everything... and he take her to a lot of places." He played with a toy car I bought him.

"Okay, help me pick out some shoes you think she will like." I told him. I bought her a pair of burgundy Airmaxes and we left the store.

I dropped him off and put her shoes in with his without telling her I had bought her anything. We said an awkward goodbye and I left her house. I was there for only a few minutes and got up out of there.

I didn't think she was talking to him about us, but he did have an idea of what we were supposed to be doing with and for one another. We would have to sit him down and explain our situation to him soon.

Carla

Kevin buying some shoes was nothing new. He had bought me plenty of gifts not just over the years but since he and Shanetta had gotten together especially. I figured he felt he had to do it to make up for how the situation was turning out. I tried the shoes on, then put them in my closet with the rest of my shoes which he had bought damn near every pair of.

Kalvin told me they had talked about what mommies and daddies are suppose to do for each other. So, I was curious. "What did Daddy tell you about Shanetta?"

"Ummm… he said, some kids are lucky to have two moms or dads or both. I'm lucky." He smiled wide and went back to playing with his toy car.

While the shit irked my nerves, it never crossed my mind to say anything out the way about Shanetta. True, I did hate that bitch's guts… but she had always been good to my son. From day one, she had treated him like her own. I respected that. "You want another daddy too?" I meant the question sarcastically, but of course at four, it went over his head.

"Nope, Daddy is the best!" He said proudly.

Yes, the fuck he is, I thought to myself. I kissed his head. "Okay. Go watch television in your room until I come get you to get in the tub."

"Okay, Mommy." He was looking more and more like his father by the day.

I poured myself a glass of wine and sat at my kitchen table. I had been acting as if the only thing I needed from Keno was dick but deep down, I had settled for fucking him just to keep a piece of him. My heart wouldn't let me accept that we were over. Not when I was still very much in love with his fine ass. He was a liar and a cheater; but he was mine. At least he had been for most of my life. *Maybe it was time for me to move on and find a new daddy for both me and Kalvin.*

The thought alone made me feel disloyal. When I left him, it was never to be with anyone else. It was to teach his ass a lesson; to wake him up to what was in front of him. To help him grow up a little so he could be what we needed him to be. I never expected him to run off and find my replacement.

I had been playing games and lost. I sat there wondering what I should do next when my phone rang. I looked at my screen and couldn't help smiling. I answered and walked to my bedroom, stopping by Kalvin's room to check in on him. This conversation would be just what I needed.

Shanetta

I only felt a little guilty sitting at an exclusive table in the new Italian restaurant in the city. It wasn't the money that had me back sitting across from the same nigga that almost got my ass whipped only months ago. Kevin had spent plenty of money on me over the past two years. I swear it was the way I could tell he still felt about Carla. Yes, I could tell he was trying to get over it; but the fact that it had been months and she was still laughing at me from behind his eyes was too much to carry around with me every day.

When he called, I told him how I was feeling and how I was missing my daughter and he offered to send me to get a massage if I was willing to leave work early like he thought I should. I took him up on that offer and we talked off and on for the rest of that day. Then on and off for the entire next day. Before I knew it, we had talked every day for two weeks.

So, when he asked me on this date, saying 'yes' felt like the natural next step.

He smiled at me flashing a row of straight white teeth and a single dimple in his right cheek. His chocolate skin gave me chocolate cravings and I felt myself wanting to fall for him. Even if it was just to feel something other than confused.

"Talk to me." He said. "What's on your mind?"

I looked into his eyes and felt a slight sense of relief. "Thank you." I told him. "For the massage, the conversation, this dinner and just making me feel..." I couldn't pinpoint the word I was looking for.

"Safe?" He finished my sentence.

"Yes." I sighed. *Did that confirm that I hadn't been feeling emotionally safe in my relationship?*

"You are safe with me, Shanetta. I know you're in that situation and I don't know what's keeping you there, but I consider you a good friend. If that's all we ever are, than I can accept that; but I'll be around if you need someone to talk to or a break from your life." The sincerity in his voice was refreshing since I hadn't been able to trust Keno for so long.

We sat there and talked for over an hour. I laughed for the first time in weeks and realized that moving on might not be as hard as I thought. "I'm serious. Thank you for this." I told him again as we waited for the check to come.

"My pleasure, beautiful. Thank you for giving me some time. I hope it's not too long before we can do it again and I'm glad to see you feeling at least a little better." He looked into my eyes and I actually felt butterflies.

I wasn't having another episode in the parking lot of my job, so I had opted to meet him at the restaurant instead. When he walked me to my car, I almost hoped he'd go in for a kiss. I was slightly disappointed when he didn't; but he took my hand as he said good night and I could settle for that.

The ride home was peaceful. I didn't let my mind drive me into feeling any guiltier that I did when I sat down at the table and I didn't let my heart give in to that giddy school girl feeling building up in the pit of my stomach either. I just listened to my music and sang along, happy to feel nothing at all for a while.

When I got home, I made dinner for Kevin and put his plate in the microwave. Then I ran myself a steaming hot bubble bath, grabbed my rose toy, and allowed the hot water to take me away.

I spent so much time in that bath playing that the water got cold on me. I let the water out and took a shower to get clean. By the time Keno came in, I was in bed on my way to sleep. I came so much in that bath that I was exhausted.

****

I was glad to find Shanetta already in bed when I walked in. I kissed her face and ate my dinner in the living room so I didn't disturb her sleep. I watched some ESPN and did some texting. I fell asleep on the couch for the first time ever. I didn't know if it made her feel awkward to wake up without me and find me sleeping peacefully on the couch the next morning, but it was a comfortable change for me. I woke up feeling refreshed.

She made me breakfast as usual and kissed my face on her way out. We told one another that we loved each other as we usually did and I meant it, but something was definitely missing. I could tell that she felt it too but she didn't say a word about it. *Was she really willing to let this be the way it was forever? I sure the fuck wasn't.* The question for me was only what was the best next move. All the pieces had fallen into place for me to have a lot of options. My settlement had come through and business was doing better than ever. I just had to choose who was moving forward with me.

Don't get me wrong, all the things I loved about Shanetta were still good things about her. They were still the things that made her a good look for me; but the heart wants what the heart wants. On the other hand, even though I loved Carla like I was beginning to think I would never love another woman...she had said and done some bullshit that changed the way I looked at her. Things that even if I could forgive, I could never forget. She had some major character flaws. Shit that I wouldn't have to worry about with Shanetta. I had to make a choice and soon.

Chapter 20

Shanetta

I decided to stop seeing my friend. While he did provide me with a shoulder to lean on when I was feeling at my lowest, I just wasn't ready to walk away from Keno. Yes, shit was rough but he was mine and I was going to stick beside him. Carla would just have to learn her place.

I woke up on my day off with love on my mind and every intension of making up with my man. I figured he had fallen asleep on the couch again, since he had been for the past week. I made my bed and went into the living room to ask him what he wanted for breakfast and figure out what we would be doing for the day; but he wasn't there. I checked the bathrooms even though I knew I hadn't heard the shower running when I got up and walked back into the living room. He was gone. No big deal, right? Maybe he got up early and had to make a run to the store or something.

I called his phone only to find out that his number had been changed. So, in a panic, I ran to my bedroom and checked the closet and dresser. All of his clothes were gone. Every trace that he had ever been there was gone. *This muthafucka had moved out of my house in the middle of the night! What the fuck kind of shit is that?*

Carla

That first called let me know it was real. When I answered, the only thing he said to me was, "I love you... and that's forever." I was disappointed that the conversation wasn't longer like I wanted when I saw it was him calling; he wasn't ready to sit me down and explain everything like I needed him to... but what he said was enough for that moment.

We began texting each other regularly. Talking about what had happened between us, my decision to leave when I found out I was pregnant with Kalvin and his decision to choose Shanetta when I let him know that I was ready to get back together. In the end, none of it mattered. All that mattered was that the love was still just as strong as ever and nothing and nobody could change that.

When he showed up at my house in the middle of the night, I was a little upset at first. "Kevin, I'm not going to be your side chick. You can't come here in the middle of the night expecting me to satisfy your needs, then have to watch you go back to her bed." I told him at the door.

"Carla, I'm not here for that. Just let me in. This is important. I gotta talk to you." He said and the urgency in his voice made me think something was wrong.

"Come in." I stepped aside so he could walk in. Then I turned my back to him to lock the door.

When I turned around and found him on one knee in front of me, I immediately burst into tears. I didn't even see the ring. I just saw his lips mouthing the words; 'will you marry me' and that was all I needed. I would have said 'yes' without a ring. I knew the first day I laid eyes on him way back in junior high that he was my forever.

Keno

I know you're thinking why the fuck would I do Shanetta like that after she lost her job and took me into her house after the fire. All I can say is this. It is what the fuck it is. I ain't love the girl like she loved me. I knew it and she felt it toward the end. I wanted to because she had a lot going for herself. Any nigga would be happy to have her... she just wasn't for me.

Proposing to Kalvin's mother was just the right thing to do. My son deserved the family I never had. He deserved the stability that having both of us under one roof could give. Carla deserved my loyalty after everything that I had put her through and I deserved Carla. My body was telling me she was home with all those wet dreams, my mind was confirming it by always reminding me of my feelings for her no matter what else I had going on. I just had to give in to the real.

I could have been good with Shanetta, but I would have never been happy. We could have eventually been stable but I would have never been satisfied fully. I was Carla's from the first time she let me lay her down. If you have something like that, somebody you keep running back to even when your current situation is solid, go be with them. Fuck how anybody else feels about it. It ain't even fair for y'all to be involving other people when you already know what it is. Fuck her feelings, fuck his feeling, fuck what 'they' think or have to say about it. Do what you have to do to get right with that person you love.

When it comes to relationships, there is no right or wrong way to go about it. What you see ain't always the whole story, and there ain't no one right way to see things. Sometimes, the bitch that got slapped did the provoking. Sometimes, the shit that goes unsaid is the cause of the shit that gets said. Sometimes, the reason you get cheated on is because you stopped doing the shit you did in the beginning; and sometimes, love just ain't enough. Sometimes, you're willing to wait and help your significant other grow and finding love is worth it in the end; but sometimes muthafuckas just ain't shit. Every situation is different and only you can know your best next move. That friend who can't keep a man can't give you any better advice than his hoe ass friend who hops bitch to bitch like it's an Olympic sport.

I might not be shit, but I gave up enough game here to get kicked out the player's club for life. So, one of you bitches better act right so I can finally settle down!

www.ingramcontent.com/pod-product-compliance
Lightning Source LLC
Chambersburg PA
CBHW070747180626
46818CB00007B/3028